His gaze locked on to her face and stayed there, unmoving for a few seconds, before the corner of his mouth slid into a lazy smile.

The corners of those amazing eyes crinkled slightly and the warmth of that smile seemed to heat the air between them. And at that moment his smile was for her. And her heart leapt. More than a little.

In that instant Toni knew what it felt like to be the most important and most beautiful person in the room. Heart thumping. Brain spinning. An odd and unfamiliar tension hummed down her veins. Every cell of her was suddenly alive and tuned in to the vibrations emanating from his body.

Suddenly she wanted to preen and flick her hair, to roll her shoulders back so that she could stick her chest out.

It was as if she had been dusted with instant lust powder.

Dear Reader

Parents. We love them dearly, but sometimes they pass on a heritage and family expectations that we cannot shake off—no matter how hard we try.

Antonia Baldoni knows about expectations. Toni is the fourth generation of the Baldoni family of artists to paint the portrait of the CEO of Elstrom Industries. She needs the money to help pay for her younger sister's gap year, with something left over for the university fees. Toni has taken care of her sister since their parents' death.

Only the new CEO is *not* the academic cartographer Lars Elstrom but his adventurer son Scott. Scott Elstrom has been brought back from Alaska to take over the company because his father is ill.

Scott certainly does not have time to sit around long enough to have his portrait painted! He might be the last of the line but he is not going to let two hundred years of heritage go down without a fight.

The one thing he *does* expect is that quirky and stubborn Toni Baldoni might just be the girl he needs to help him save Elstrom Mapping—and give him hope for a second chance at love.

I do hope that you enjoy travelling with Toni and Scott on their journey to discover how they can put the past behind them and move forward together to a new life.

I would love to hear from my readers, and you can get in touch by visiting www.ninaharrington.com

Nina

WHO'S AFRAID OF THE BIG BAD BOSS?

BY

NINA HARRINGTON

MILLS & BOON

Published in Great Britain 2014
by Mills & Boon, an imprint of Harlequin (UK) Limited,
Eton House, 18-24 Paradise Road, Richmond, Surrey, TW9 1SR

© 2014 Nina Harrington

ISBN: 978 0 263 91140 4

Harlequin (UK) Limited's policy is to use papers that are natural, renewable and recyclable products and made from wood grown in sustainable forests. The logging and manufacturing processes conform to the legal environmental regulations of the country of origin.

Printed and bound in Spain
by Blackprint CPI, Barcelona

Nina Harrington grew up in rural Northumberland, England, and decided at the age of eleven that she was going to be a librarian—because then she could read *all* of the books in the public library whenever she wanted! Since then she has been a shop assistant, community pharmacist, technical writer, university lecturer, volcano walker and industrial scientist, before taking a career break to realise her dream of being a fiction writer. When she is not creating stories which make her readers smile, her hobbies are cooking, eating, enjoying good wine— and talking, for which she has had specialist training.

Other Modern Tempted™ titles by Nina Harrington:

THE SECRET INGREDIENT
TROUBLE ON HER DOORSTEP

This and other titles by Nina Harrington are available in eBook format from www.millsandboon.co.uk

CHAPTER ONE

Scott Elstrom looked out across the sea ice and squinted as the Alaskan sun rose over the horizon and made the light covering of snow suddenly turn brilliantly white.

It was so beautiful that for a moment he forgave the brutal biting wind that came with crossing the frozen sea. There was no cover for himself or his team of nine sled dogs and he could feel his cheeks burning with frostbite under the mask covering his face.

Reaching up with gloved hands, Scott turned off his head torch to save the batteries and, stepping off the sled, he ran a hundred paces on the thick plate of ice to get some warmth into his body and then jumped back onto the sled, much to the amusement of the dogs. The lead dog, Dallas, actually looked back and seemed to grin at him.

The dogs loved this weather: bright sunshine and a clear trail ahead across the sound to the base camp on the other side of the bay.

The fact that they had only crossed this stretch of sea ice once before didn't matter. They were happy just to be out and doing what they did best. *Running.*

He had been out with his dogs for thirteen days, taking mapping and geo readings at each of the twenty stations the ecological survey company had established. Some-times that meant staying in a small town along the way but often the station was a simple wooden house or shack where he would be alone with his dogs, checking their feet and feeding them. He loved this way of life and the gentle routine that they had settled into.

Out here in the silence he felt a kinship with all of the explorers who had used Elstrom maps in the past to find a route to new worlds as well as to hunt and fish.

Now that routine was shattered. The message from his sister, Freya, had been short and to the point.

Their father was in hospital. He had suffered another stroke and, although it was a small one and the doctors said that he should make a good recovery, his father wanted to talk to him. Urgently. *Come home, Scott. We need you here.*

Scott rolled his shoulders and fought back a sense of guilt at his resentment at having to go back to what passed for civilization a week earlier than he had planned.

They needed him. *Well, that was new!*

It had been two years since his father had handed over the management of their family business to his stepbrother, Travis. And look how well that decision had turned out! Now Travis was long gone and his father had been fighting for months to save what was left of Elstrom Mapping.

For their father to even admit that he needed Scott was astonishing.

That was why Scott had taken the decision to cross the open water instead of travelling inland and taking the slower route through the frozen forest and rivers to the station where he would find a snow machine and a lift to the local airstrip.

There was no other choice. He had to cross the frozen sea ice to get to the base camp to the airbase in time to catch the weekly cargo plane—it would take too long any other way.

But crossing open salt water ice was a serious commitment. The sea froze in huge cracked and floating plates which moved and heaved under the sled, making progress slow and dangerous. The ice was always unstable and never more so in the unusually mild Alaskan February.

Scott looked over the sled and, to his horror, he could see the ice ridges flexing and cracking. A giant piece of ice had broken away and was floating out to sea. He was driving across the frozen-over thinner layer.

One crack in a weak spot and the weight of the sled would drag him and the whole dog team underwater to their deaths, never to be found again.

There was a low grunt from his lead dog, Dallas, as she picked up a scent and set off at a steady pace onto the thicker ice, the other eight dogs behind her panting and settling into a trot from months of training and working together. They would run all day if he asked them, without complaint.

The blinding sunlight made Scott squint and glance sideways towards the open water of the sea.

For the last twenty-four hours he had been travelling and had barely dozed in the wooden trappers' cabin for the the four or five hours while the dogs rested. Now, as the sun rose higher and warmed his skin, and the dogs moved steadily forwards, his mind drifted seawards.

The only sound was from the movement of the sled on the ice and the comforting panting noises of nine dogs moving as a team.

Beautiful. Unique. *Mesmerising.*

This was his life now. Not central London and everything that went with it.

He had waved goodbye to that world two years ago and would quite happily not see it again unless he had to. The technology he was using for his mapping and surveying meant that he could talk to his sister and his father, if he chose to, most days and at least once a week.

Of course Freya had tried to persuade him to come home for Christmas but what had been the point?

His quiet academic father had never understood how his son preferred adventure sports and a hard outdoor life to the quiet study of the maps and charts that had made Elstrom Mapping a familiar name around the world.

The only common thing holding them together had been the mapping company, and when his father had decided that Travis could be trusted to lead the company that link had been swept away, leaving nothing but regrets and harsh words behind.

The weather had closed in during December and made travel impossible for anyone at the research station, so he had a perfectly valid and very convenient excuse to stay in Alaska.

Way too convenient an excuse according to his sister, who'd ended up coping on her own for the holidays, being bounced between divorced parents who had drifted away from one another for years before their mother finally gave up trying to make a family with a father who was never home. Freya had spent New Year's with their quite happily settled mother and her new boyfriend—a lawyer with a fine selection of colourful bow ties.

Scott chuckled to himself deep in the back of his throat. Freya would make him suffer for that one. He looked up and was just about to check his GPS position when his world shifted.

He felt the sled shudder and slip underneath him.

They had hit a weak spot in the ice.

Instantly every cell in his body leapt to attention, adrenaline surging through his veins.

While he had been thinking about London firesides, Dallas had slowed down, her tail high and in the shape of a question mark instead of hanging straight down. And her paws were dancing.

Scott's heart almost stopped.

He couldn't swim in five layers of thermal clothing and, even if he could, the water was so cold he wouldn't last more than a few minutes. He would go down with the sled and the dogs.

The dogs would die because his father had given up the fight.

No way. Not while he still had breath in his body.

Scott snatched up the solid grab rope and dropped off the back of the sled onto his stomach, his legs spread wide so his body weight would be spread over the thin ice. 'Dallas. Gee right. Gee right. Dallas.'

Dallas knew that this was the instruction to turn right to safety and she tugged and tugged as the team fought her, the other eight dogs desperate to run hard and straight. But she did it and after a few terrifying minutes Scott felt a ridge of hard ice under his stomach and they were back on the older solid pan ice.

The broken shards of ice ripped his right glove to shreds and his fingers instantly turned numb and blue. Frostbite. But he managed to haul himself back onto the sled and the dogs sped on to safety as the shapes of the cabins on the other side of the bay grew clearer in the growing early morning light.

He was going to make it home in time to hear what his father had to say after all.

But one thing was for sure. This was his chance to prove to his father that he was a better man than Travis could ever be. And nothing was going to stand in his way and stop him from making that happen. Not this time.

* * *

'So let me get this straight. Those G-strings are edible?'

Toni pulled away the wrapping paper from the pink and black gift box that her sister Amy had given her and started reading the instructions on the back.

'Of course.' Amy shrugged and flicked the fluffy feather end of her pink whip against the packing. 'Why else would you want to wear something that uncomfortable?'

'I have just had a vision of what happens when those candy pieces come adrift and where they might end up in my lady parts. Amy, I love you and you are my only sister but I may save modelling this particular birthday pressie for another day.'

Amy giggled and shook her head. 'Those knickers are not for us to ogle at. Save it for that hunky boyfriend you're going to meet.' She knocked her on the head with the feather whip again. 'Very soon.'

'Well, in that case I might as well put the box in the freezer right now and stick to eating supermarket chocolate bars.'

Amy sighed out loud and collapsed down on the arm of the dining chair next to Toni. 'Now don't be like that. It has been a whole year since you got rid of that skanky Peter and what did we agree? He was totally not worthy of your luscious magnificence. Right? Of course right. This is a new year and a new you, remember?'

Toni smiled and hugged the present to her new burgundy satin bra. 'When did you get to be so clever? I'm going to miss having you around. You know that, don't you?'

'Of course. That's why I've loaded up all these fancy gizmos on my tech so that we can talk every week!'

Amy wrapped one arm around Toni's bare shoulders

and rocked from side to side. 'It's only a few months and I'll be right back in time to start university in September.' Then she slid back and sniffed once. 'And, for the record, I'll miss you too but I'll work hard to block out my pain by having the best gap year trip this world has to offer.'

Then she pointed the whip at Toni. 'All thanks to the lovely Christmas present from my darling sister.' She nodded over her shoulder. 'The gals still cannot believe that you bought me a round-the-world plane ticket. Magic!'

'How else could I get you out of the house long enough to get the plumbing fixed?' Toni grinned. 'You're welcome. But you do remember that there's one condition. You have to enjoy yourself and not spend the whole time digging up bits of ancient Peru.'

'I can guarantee it. Oh! Looks like I'm getting the signal. I think more birthday cake might be almost ready. Be back soon.'

And with that Amy got to her feet and sashayed off as though she always wore a black laced-up pink and cream frilly basque and feather-trimmed mules around the house.

Toni sat back in her hard wooden chair and swayed a little from side to side as her whole crew of pals and colleagues from the media company where she worked joined in a very loud and very out of tune version of an old hit song about an uptown girl which was playing at full volume in her honour.

There was cheap Prosecco and white wine spillages and pizza and cheesy biscuit breadcrumbs all over the tablecloth, and probably the new plum lingerie that Amy had squeezed her into as the star of her Birthday Goddess sexy party special. At some point she had lost her shoe under the table when she sat down after all the toasts had been made.

Then Amy had presented her with a crown she had

made from gold paper and wire and insisted that she wear it as a party princess. At a jaunty angle, of course.

Worse. Her make-up was probably a wreck after a brief but intense crying jag when Amy had said some incredibly sweet things about how lucky she was to have her as her sister and that leaving home for the first time was not going to change a thing.

The waterworks had started again when Amy gave her a bound book of their mother's sketches of them as children and told her how proud their late parents would have been of her and what she had achieved, which had everyone in the room reaching for the tissues, paper napkins or, in more than one case, the corner of the tablecloth. There was not a dry eye in the house. Even Amy the Strong 'accidentally' dropped her napkin on the floor and had to drop out of sight for a couple of minutes to find it.

Good thing that the birthday chocolate iced cupcakes had arrived just in time to prevent a meltdown of nuclear proportions.

Toni glanced up across the tables and clusters of women spread out around the room. It didn't matter that she looked a mess and that her guests were in great danger of trashing the dining and living room of a house she was borrowing from Freya Elstrom. Not to her friends, who had come out on a cold February evening to help her celebrate her birthday.

Amy had a lot to answer for. She had told Amy for weeks that she did not want a birthday party. It would only remind her of what had happened on her last birthday, when she had found her so-called boyfriend in the shower with the Brazilian lingerie model who turned out to be his real full-time girlfriend.

The one he had so conveniently forgotten to mention

during the previous few weeks when he had been dating her.

That had not been one of her life's finer moments.

Especially since she had already stripped off and was ready to make sure that Peter was washed in all of his important places.

Hence this surprise party. Toni's latest project had been staging professional studio photo sessions on the explosion in demand for sex toys and bedroom accessories and daring lingerie among women of all ages. Young and old.

When Toni had mentioned it was her birthday in a few days *and* the first anniversary of breaking up with her cheating boyfriend then the girls had insisted that they hold a party for her to mark the occasion while Amy was still in London. Complete with the full range of accessories which had been used on the show. Amy thought this was a great idea and had arranged the whole thing while Toni was at work.

These were her real friends. Her real family. Girls from the local school she had known all of her life, who had left their husbands and boyfriends at home for one evening to share her birthday party, pals from her work, students from Amy's school. All loud, boisterous and having fun. And that was precisely how she liked it. No false pretenses here. Real people who shared her life each and every day.

She was so lucky to have them.

And she was officially on holiday for two weeks. Now that was worth celebrating. Even if she would be spending most of the time painting the company portrait of a very serious-looking businessman. According to his daughter Freya, Dr Lars Elstrom was a quiet academic used to desk work and she had talked him into sitting for his portrait while he was in the office researching some work for a client.

But there was a problem. The painting had to be painted in a specific two-week window in February before her father went back to Italy for the spring. Could she do it?

Piece of cake.

Especially when the cake came decorated with half the fee for the commission in advance.

Thank you, Freya, and thank you, Dr Lars Elstrom.

That fee had bought Amy's round-the-world plane ticket *and* was paying to have the boiler replaced in her little house. Hot water! Central heating she could rely on! Bliss. Apparently any tenant thinking of renting her house would expect plumbing that worked. Amazing. Some people had no appreciation of character properties.

Toni glanced out of the dining room window at the flurries of February snow which were forecast to be with them for a few days to come. Not the weather to be modelling fancy lingerie in her freezing terraced house. It might only be thirty minutes away on foot but it might as well be in another world. *Brr.*

No. Much better to do it here in this nice warm house.

Freya had a lovely home and Toni was going to enjoy living here for the next two weeks rent-free. And with all of the hot water she could use.

She loved patrons who believed in carrying on old traditions! Especially when that tradition meant that the CEO of the company always had their portrait painted by a Baldoni. And since she was the last in the line… Result!

A warm glow of happiness and contentment spread from deep inside her like a furnace that pumped the heat from her heart to the very ends of her fingertips. She had not felt so safe and secure for years. Protected. And cared for and part of a very special community of friends who looked out for one another.

She grinned across at Amy's best friend, Lucy, who

was demonstrating the finer points of how to tie a sarong. They had known one another since they were at primary school together just a few streets away. It was hard to imagine that Amy, Lucy and the other girls parading up and down in various stages of undress would be flying out tomorrow, all ready for trekking through rough terrain in South America.

It was actually happening. Her baby sister was going around the world with her best friends. One month travelling. Four months on an archaeological dig in Peru then another month relaxing. Six months. Three girls. Three boys. All great teenagers she had known for years. But six months? The longest they had lived apart since their parents died was over a year ago, when she'd worked in Paris for five weeks but came home most weekends.

They might have had the training and they all spoke excellent Spanish but the hard reality of what they would be facing made her shudder.

But no sniffles allowed. Time to start living a bit. Right? That was what they'd agreed at some mad hour on New Year's Day. A new start for both of them. Pity that Amy was insisting that a new boyfriend was part of the package.

Maybe turning twenty-seven was not so bad after all when she had friends like these in her life. So what if she didn't have a mega career as a fine artist? She had something much better.

And somehow she knew that her father would understand that trying to scrape a living as a portrait painter had never been the life she wanted and never would be. That had been her father's dearest wish, but it wasn't hers. No. This portrait for Freya Elstrom would be the last. No more commissions as the last of the Baldoni family. It was time to say goodbye to foolish ideas like that and start focusing totally on her photography career.

Amy sashayed forward with a plate with a cupcake on and leant sideways and rested her head on Toni's shoulder. 'I stashed two of the red velvet specials, which I happen to know are your favourite, in the washing machine.'

'Clever!' Toni replied and popped a little finger loaded with creamy chocolate icing into her mouth and groaned in delight. 'Delish. And have I said thank you yet again for arranging all of this? It's amazing and I love it.'

Amy laughed out loud and gave her a one-armed hug. 'Several times. It's the wine, you know. Causes short-term memory loss in older women.'

Then Amy started rubbing her hands together and mumbling under her breath. 'Now. Back to the important stuff. What totally outrageous thing have you decided to do while I'm away? Remember the rules—it has to be spontaneous, the opposite of what you would normally do, and fun! Points will be awarded for the most ingenious solution!'

'Dance on the table? Toni suggested then shook her head and waved her arms around. 'No. Forget that one. The table legs wouldn't cope with my current body weight and this food is too good to waste. Something outrageous. Um...'

Then she looked over Amy's shoulder back towards the door leading to the hallway and her breath caught in her throat.

Standing not ten feet away from her was one of the most remarkable-looking men that she had seen in her life.

She was five foot nine so he had to be at least six foot two, from his heavy working boots and quilted jacket to the black cap pulled low over long, crazily curled dirty blond hair.

Slim hips. Broad shoulders. Long legs.

Her gaze tracked up his body before the sensible part of her brain clicked in to stop it.

'Oh, Amy—' she breathed in a low hiss of appreciation '—I owe you big time.'

'This is so true! But what particular thing have I done now?' Amy replied between mouthfuls of cake.

'You didn't tell me that you hired a lumberjack male stripper.'

'Who? What?' Amy looked up and whirled her head around like a meerkat before it froze in the same direction Toni was focusing on.

'Oh. I see what you mean,' she said with a cough and started taking photographs with the small digital camera that Toni carried with her everywhere.

'I have no idea who that is and he is nothing to do with me, but what are you waiting for? Go and find out who he belongs to and if he's available—nab him for yourself before any of the other gals do.'

And with that Amy pranced off towards her friends in her frilly lace-trimmed corset, which was going to be of zero value on an archaeological excavation in the Andes.

Leaning against the door frame, the mystery man didn't move an inch. The very tall, very rugged, very cold-looking mystery man.

He was a fashion stylist's idea of what would pass for an Indiana Jones style adventurer—after the action. In fact she would go so far as to say that he was quite scruffy.

Conscious that she was standing there ogling his long denim-clad legs, Toni's gaze ratcheted up to his face just as he glanced in her direction. Blue eyes gazed at her so intently from under heavy dark blond eyebrows that she almost blushed under the fierce heat of that focus.

With cheekbones that sharp he could have passed for
a male model if it was not for the heavy, definitely non-
designer dirty blond and grey beard and the blue strapping
that was bandaged around his right hand. His clothing was
practical. Stained and well used. If this was a costume then
it was entirely authentic!

He had not said one word to anyone but in those eyes
and on that powerful face she recognised something very
special. Confidence oozed out of every pore of this man's
body. He knew exactly who he was and what he wanted
and what he was doing there.

That must be nice!

The way he simply leant against the door frame enjoying the view, as though he walked into a lingerie party
every day of the week, screamed someone who was so
totally comfortable in his own skin that it was sickening.

While she was dressed in a tiny purple satin push-up
bra and matching shorts.

Oh, what? Not funny. So not funny.

Toni grabbed her kimono from the back of the sofa
and pushed her arms into the sleeves faster than she'd
thought possible!

Okay, some of these girls were used to wearing lingerie in front of the camera for a living, but she wasn't. She
didn't like the idea that some stranger was standing there
getting a good eyeful of a catwalk show.

Wait a minute. What the hell was he doing here? And
who had invited him? Freya never said anything about
having a boyfriend.

Perhaps he was just passing and someone left the door
open!

'Man alert!' Toni cupped her hands around her mouth
and yelled, 'Unaccompanied male in the room, girls!'

The screaming and squealing had to be heard to be believed.

Utter chaos erupted on all sides as the girls scattered to the wind, mostly upstairs to the bedrooms from the sound of it.

Righty. Time to sort this out.

Toni narrowed her eyes and pulled the edges of her kimono tighter together.

She tried to stomp over to the hulk but it was a tad tricky in feather mules so she ended up mincing across the room instead. Head high, chin forward.

And those blue eyes focused on every tiny step she took.

She cleared her throat and looked him straight in the eye.

'Okay. You look like the kind of guy who likes straight talk. I'm Antonia Baldoni, house guest of Freya Elstrom. This—' and she waved one hand towards the abandoned articles and some very odd bedroom toys '—is my birthday party. And you are?'

He moved slightly away from the wall to an almost upright position so that when he spoke the sound came from several inches above her head.

'Tired. Hungry. Surprised. And delighted to make your acquaintance, Antonia Baldoni. House guest.' He rolled back his shoulders and exhaled very slowly through his nose. 'Strange. I've just come from Freya and she never mentioned anything about a house guest.'

There was a definite squeak and a giggle from behind Toni's back and one side of this man's mouth twitched just once before he breathed, 'Make that house guests. And just when I thought this day could not get any more bizarre.'

'You've just seen Freya?' Toni looked at him with her

eyes narrowed and her head tilted to one side. 'Really? You have to forgive me, but I find that a little hard to believe. Freya was invited to my party tonight but sent her apologies from Italy. So. Perhaps it's time for you to start talking before I throw you out. Let's start with the big ones. Where exactly did you say you met Freya? And what are you doing here? And who are you?'

A low thundering sigh rumbled low in this big man's chest and Toni stepped back as he slung his body forward as though it was taking a huge effort and strode past her into the kitchen, looking around as he did so from side to side, leaving an aroma in his wake which made her waft the air with one hand.

'Hey. Wait a minute. I didn't invite you in,' Toni said and shuffled after him in her mules.

'You don't have to,' the blond said and pointed to a framed photo on the wall between the cabinets. It was one of a collection of what looked like holiday snaps which Toni had not had time to admire. Until now.

By going up on tiptoe Toni could get a better look at what seemed to be a family photo of people gathered around a dinner table. She recognised Freya and an older man who looked so much like her that he had to be her father, Lars Elstrom. And standing behind them, grinning for the camera, was a tall handsome blond man with broad shoulders and blue eyes the same colour as...

She whipped around, blinked at the man standing with his arms folded and then back to the photo.

Her shoulders dropped. He nodded very slowly up and down. Once.

'Scott Elstrom. Freya's brother. And I live here.'

Then he sniffed and gestured with his head towards the worktop. 'Is anyone going to eat that pizza?'

Toni stared at the photograph and then glanced up at the serious expression on his face before returning back to the framed snapshot of the man, scowling at her at some sort of winter sporting event.

It was definitely him. No mistaking the dirty blond hair and physique.

It was definitely on Freya's kitchen wall.

And, just like that, the effects of two hours of wine-drinking and general merriment popped like an over-stretched balloon and what was left of the rational part of her brain kicked right back in.

Not a male stripper.

Not a birthday present in the shape of a hunky lumberjack.

He was Freya Elstrom's brother.

Nightmare!

Toni closed her eyes and pinched the top of her nose. She gestured back towards the party, which had magically returned to full swing inside the dining room, with the flat of her hand. 'As you can see, this is my birthday party. And I'm rather occupied at present.'

His slightly bloodshot blue eyes locked onto hers. 'I'm not going anywhere.'

At this distance all she could focus on were the thin pale tan lines radiating out from the corners of his eyes and the dark stubble and grey-blond beard above that full, sensuous upper lip.

But there was nothing polished about this man. Far from it. His cheeks looked more sunburnt than tanned and his jacket and trousers were designed for hard use and had seen it. Unshaven. Unkempt.

Inhaling was a mistake. He smelt of leather and travel and acrid sweat mixed with wet dog in a combination which perfume manufacturers could bottle as instant girl-repellent.

Smelly did not quite cover it. This man was seriously in need of a long soak and a shave and several cans of deodorant.

Then the right side of his mouth turned up into what was probably meant to be a reassuring smile.

And every sensory switch inside her body turned on to maximum power.

Just like that. Completely out of the blue and totally, totally not what she wanted to happen. *Especially not now.*

Speech was impossible and for what seemed like minutes, but was probably only seconds, they both stood there in silence. Breathing in air which positively crackled with electricity. Neither of them willing to shift an inch.

It was almost a relief when someone's mobile phone started ringing. The ringtone was the theme song for a popular Italian coffee shop. Amy had been playing with it earlier that day; she loved coffee and wasn't sure when she would see her next cappuccino.

'I think it's yours.' He blinked, breaking the connection, stepping back and folding his arms.

Toni turned away and sucked in some air because apparently she had stopped breathing. She reached into the tiny evening bag she had left on the kitchen worktop and found the phone in the inside pocket, flipping open the tiny, silver, high-tech unit as a familiar voice hissed down the line.

'Sorry to interrupt, but are you coming back in?' Amy whispered. 'Lucy is just about to light the candles on the birthday cake and we're frightened of the fire risk. You can bring the hunk with you if you'd like to help.'

'Be right there,' she replied and closed the phone.

Sucking in a long breath, Toni lifted her head and stared

into the face of one of the strangest-looking men she had ever met in her life.

Hell. Who was she kidding? He was smelly, bandaged and glaring at her. And totally gorgeous.

'Stay right where you are. Help yourself to the pizza. I'll be back soon and we can sort all of this out.'

CHAPTER TWO

HUSTLING A GAGGLE of still giggling party girls into their clothes proved more difficult than Toni had imagined, especially when their unexpected male guest was trapped in the kitchen and they were all desperate to take another peek before they left.

In the end Amy came to her rescue with the vague excuse that it was getting late and some of them had an early plane to catch. The next ten minutes were a mad rush of tidying up, distributing the bedroom toys and assorted lingerie items into party bags and arguments about whether they should break into the kitchen to rescue the chocolate brownies they had saved for the coffee.

It was almost a relief when she finally kissed Amy goodnight with promises that she would call if there was any trouble, and finally waved the girls goodbye from the doorstep.

Toni dropped her head back against the heavy door and gazed down the hallway towards the kitchen.

Trouble was waiting for her behind that innocent white-painted door. She just didn't know how much.

Swallowing down a huge lump of apprehension, Toni inhaled a couple of short, sharp breaths. Perhaps she shouldn't have downed all of those mystery cocktails Lucy had concocted followed by the champagne and wine.

Probably.

Blinking hard, she pushed away from the front door with the flat of both hands. Time to find out what Scott Elstrom was doing back in town.

Casually pushing the door open, Toni sauntered into the kitchen with as much aplomb as she could muster.

Scott was sitting on a bar stool with his back against the kitchen wall and an empty plate in front of him.

He had stripped off his outer coat and hung it from a hook near the back door that Toni had not even noticed before. *Um.* Maybe he had been here before?

'How was the pizza?' she asked in a sing-song voice as she took in the heavy grey and blond beard and dark blond hair. 'If you fancy dessert, why don't you help yourself to the chocolate willy lollipops? There are several flavours and they are anatomically correct.'

He scowled at them and coughed. 'That's good to know but I'll pass.' Then he nodded to the brownie pan. 'Those look good.'

Toni clutched the tray and slid it across the worktop out of his reach. 'My finest recipe. Which my birthday party guests would have enjoyed if the party had not been broken up so early by an unexpected guest. These brownies are staying over here until I have a few more answers.'

'I didn't ask you to send the girls home. As for unexpected—' he raised his bandaged right hand in the air '—no clue you were going to be here. No apologies. No excuses. And those brownies do smell good.'

'No brownie until I know who you really are,' she replied with a shake of her head and folded her arms. 'That's only one photo. You could be some distant freeloading relative who Freya doesn't want sleeping in her spare room. Or some ex-boyfriend. Or something.'

Without saying another word, he lifted a smartphone

out of a side pocket on the leg of his cargo trousers, placed it on the breakfast bar and started tapping away. Toni couldn't help but notice that his body might be on the sinewy side but his fingers were long and slender.

'Hiya. Yes, I got here. How are things? Really? He's already asking for pen and paper? Unbelievable...yes, I know.' Then he shot her a glance. 'By the way, I've just met your house-sitter. She gave me pizza and is ready to call the police to get rid of the crazy vagrant who thinks he lives here. Now don't be like that. Calm down. You've had a few other things on your mind these past few days. Take a deep breath. That's better. Inhale slowly. It's all under control. Now, why don't you have a word with your pal while I eat her brownies, okay? Okay.'

Toni could only watch, stunned, as this tall man in a check shirt turned around on the bar stool and calmly stretched out his hand towards her. 'It's for you. My sister would like a word.'

Five minutes later Toni collapsed down on the bar stool opposite Scott in a complete daze.

'I am so sorry. We had no idea or we would never have organised a birthday party while your dad is in the hospital. Wow. That is so inappropriate I don't know where to start.'

She reached into the brownie tin and cut an enormous cube and started nibbling at it to try and calm her nerves.

'We had absolutely no clue. Because I would definitely have cancelled if Freya had let me know. Seriously. I would. This is awful. I feel so embarrassed. Mortified, really. That is all so inappropriate. Please let me apologise again and...'

Scott held up one hand. 'I get it. You didn't know. It's your birthday. So you organised a party and enjoyed yourself. No problem.'

'Actually, my birthday isn't until Thursday but my sister Amy is leaving on a gap year trip tomorrow and she wanted to help me celebrate before she left so she arranged this surprise party and all my friends from the company turned up and… I am babbling. Because I am mega embarrassed.'

'That would be true. About the babbling.'

Toni took another nibble of brownie before daring to glance up at this man who was just sitting there in silence, dominating the space.

'So you are not a male stripper. Sorry about that little confusion. It was a ladies only night so any man had to have a very good reason for being there. And, seeing as none of the girls claimed you…I might have jumped to the wrong conclusion.'

His mouth opened slightly as though he was about to reply, then he reconsidered and closed it again. A rough-skinned hand rasped over his beard and he glanced quickly over his clothing as his voice rasped low in his throat. 'You thought that I was a male stripper? What kind of stripper turns up dressed like this?'

She winced and closed one eye and pretended to duck slightly.

'Scruffy lumberjack. Check shirt. Beard. Very popular with the city girls who like a—' she coughed quickly '—less refined country look.'

Then she blinked. 'The oiled chest and man string are a bit old-fashioned these days. The hunky bit of rough… oh, I didn't mean to say…imply that you're rough or anything, but…'

'Maybe you ought to stop talking now. I am not the oiled chest type even on a good day and this has not been one of them.'

'Oh. Yes. Right. Good. Or not good, depending on how bad your day has been. If you know what I mean.'

'How bad has it been? Let me see.'

His dark blond eyebrows squeezed tight together and he pinched his forehead with a thumb and middle finger.

'Almost lost a hand to frostbite. A pig of a snow machine to an air base. Cargo plane from Alaska to Iceland, scheduled flight to Rome, where I had to pay first class to get a seat, four hours at a hospital trying to work out what the hell was happening then a flight back to London. And don't get me started with how long it took me to get from the airport to the hospital and back again.'

He lifted his chin and dropped his hand away.

'So, overall, I'm not too happy about being here right now. I think that would sum it up.'

Toni blew out fast through narrowed lips. 'Alaska? In February? Frostbite? Well, that explains a lot.'

Then she slipped off the breakfast bar stool and flicked out both of her hands. 'Righty. What would you like? Coffee or tea? And I can easily reheat these brownies for you. Oh—you've already eaten the last of them. No problem, there are plenty more in the freezer. It will only take twenty minutes tops.'

He replied by easing his weight off the bar stool and rolling back his shoulders, making his chest pop.

'Thanks for the offer, but it's late and my body clock is deep-fried. Nice to meet you and thanks for the unexpected entertainment but I'm heading to bed. If you're here in the morning we might try to have a conversation which isn't in code. But right now I am way too tired to talk about the why and how.'

Then he looked up at her and asked, 'The bedroom with the blue door—I usually keep it locked. Anyone sleeping in there?'

'Oh, no. Still locked. Freya said it was private.'

And, with a quick nod in her direction, Toni watched him sling the huge duffel bag over one shoulder with a grunt and a wince. The weight of it meant that he had to lean forward from the waist but he shifted the load a few times before striding into the hallway and to the staircase which led to the bedrooms.

It took a few seconds for her champagne and wine-fuddled brain to connect with what was going on.

Her commission! Oh, no!

'Wait a minute. One last question. I'm supposed to stay with Freya for another week and work with her father at the Elstrom office. Do I need to reschedule? I mean…when will your father be back in London?'

His steps slowed and with one movement he lowered the duffel on to the hall carpet. There was something in the way his shoulders were braced tight that made Toni feel the heat of his gaze even before he looked sideways at her.

Her body locked into a half-in-the-hallway-half-in-the-kitchen position. She simply couldn't move. It was as if her feet were reluctant to leave the relative safety of the kitchen, just in case.

'News flash. I'm back. Freya's in Italy. Dad won't be coming back any time soon. As of today, he has officially retired. Goodbye Elstrom Mapping. Hello Italy.'

Then he gave a twitch. 'Sorry. But it looks like you're out of a job.'

His gaze scanned her scantily clad body from the toes sticking out from the feathery mules to the top of her gold paper crown and lingering at all of the right places on the way up.

The start of a lazy lopsided smile warmed his mouth. 'No rush to get packed tonight. Tomorrow will do. Goodnight.'

* * *

Goodnight? Out of a job? What?

Any lingering after-effects of the party had gone in a flash.

Before Scott could start up the stairs, Toni dashed in front of him and stood on the bottom step so that they were at more or less the same height.

To his credit, Scott Elstrom didn't even flinch but braced himself, legs apart, and stared at her as she crossed her arms and stared him out.

'Oh, no, you don't. I signed a contract with Freya Elstrom to paint a portrait of the CEO of Elstrom Mapping. She was the one who got in contact with me. Begging me to do the work. I've dropped everything to be here.'

There was a deep low sigh from the man standing only inches in front of her and he shifted his gaze from her face to the wall for a few seconds.

'What was your surname again?'

'Baldoni. Ah, I can see that you recognise it. The Baldoni family have painted the last four generations of Elstrom chairmen. Freya called me just after Christmas to set it up for her father. Apparently he had been thinking about it for a while and finally just decided to go ahead with his portrait. This is the earliest I could do it, which makes me feel sick.'

'Christmas. Right. So she asked you to paint his portrait after the holidays. No wonder she wanted me there.'

'Actually, she was more concerned that it was a Baldoni than which member of my family it was. Apparently your father is a stickler for tradition.'

'You might say that,' he murmured and ran his hand back through his dirty blond, very scraggy hair. 'He would want the same artist if he could do it.'

'Tricky, since my grandfather is long gone. But if Mr

Elstrom is ill,' she murmured to herself, and then realised that Scott was still listening, 'of course I can reschedule the sitting. That's not a problem. When your father is better, Freya can let me know. I have some photos that she sent me and I'm sure I can come up with something he will be pleased with... Why are you shaking your head? Is there something else?'

'My father is retired, Miss Baldoni. As of this afternoon, I am the new head of Elstrom Mapping.'

His eyebrows squeezed closer together but his gaze focused laser-sharp on her face.

'And the last thing I need is my portrait painted.'

Scott stood back and watched the fiery brunette with the lovely brown eyes stomp past him up the staircase towards the guest bedroom before picking up his over-heavy duffel.

Toni Baldoni probably had no idea how much he enjoyed following her up the stairs. One slow step at a time.

The last time he had shared this house with girls wearing nothing but lingerie had been on Freya's university graduation party, when he had dared to turn up an hour early and walked in on way too many over-excited girls high on champagne and life, all fighting for the hair straighteners and his attention. They had even taken over his en suite bathroom to cope with the party preparations.

Strange. He hadn't thought about that in a long time.

An unexpected quiver of a laugh surprised him as this brunette stomped in her ridiculous shoes down the landing and her light gown wafted up, giving him a delightful flash of creamy thigh.

Eyes flashing, she instantly flung a glance at him over one shoulder and tugged down her gown, shot into the guest room and shut the door very firmly behind her.

Shaking his head and blinking to stay awake, Scott

found the key, turned it in the lock and stepped inside the same bedroom that he had claimed the very first day he had arrived with Freya and his mother. This clean and uncluttered modern town house had seemed like another world from the dark, creaky old Victorian stone villa that was the family home they had shared with their father.

Sheer force of habit made him drop his duffel bag next to the bed and unlock and fling open the double windows to let some air into the overheated and stuffy room.

He didn't need the heat.

He just wanted sleep and quiet to process the events of the day.

Freya had known that he wasn't planning to come back any time soon and not that much had changed in the two years since he had last slept here.

It looked like the same bed, wardrobe and furnishings that he remembered.

But there was something new. Perched on the window ledge was a silver-framed photograph of a stunningly pretty slim blonde in a flimsy summer dress with legs that went on for ever.

Alexa.

Scott picked up the frame and glanced at it for a second before stashing it in the drawer of the bedside cabinet.

He had taken the photograph that first summer holiday they spent together walking in Switzerland. They were both single, in their twenties and had the whole world ahead of them.

In his eyes Alexa was the perfect woman for him. As a teenager he had watched his very different parents drift apart over the years and lead separate lives until the only thing they had in common was Freya and himself.

He wouldn't make that mistake.

Alexa was clever, stunningly pretty and, best of all,

a total sports fanatic like himself. They used to talk for hours about the things they both loved, laughing over tall tales from all of the exotic places that they had visited. They had been inseparable.

Heady with the mountain air, they had fallen in love. Over the next twelve months, they were so caught up in their engagement and the whirlwind of a top London wedding that he didn't have time to stop and consider what married life was going to be like.

It was hard to believe that it could have ended so badly.

If Freya thought that being reminded of happier times with Alexa would help him to get over his cheating ex-wife then she didn't understand.

There were some things a sunny disposition couldn't fix.

Sometimes betrayal went too deep, like a bullet to the chest which lay too close to vital organs to be removed. Always there. Always catching you out when you least expected it.

A flash of memory surged through his brain, hot and wild. He could almost see Alexa reclining on this same bed, with a look of love in her eyes, beckoning him to join her. Her long straight blonde hair that he used to adore spread out across the pillow, warm, soft and inviting.

The frostbite in his fingers was nothing compared to this type of deep-seated pain.

Scott's fingers tightened around the edge of the window frame as he looked out into the night sky, which in London was never going to be truly dark or clear.

Closing his eyes for a second, he gave way to the surge of anger and disappointment that he had buried deep inside himself since the moment he had walked into that hospital room in Rome.

It had been one of the most humbling experiences of

his life. It was astonishing to see his father looking so low and depressed. Lars Elstrom had given up. Stopped trying. Beaten down by the events of the past few years to the point where he didn't even see any point in keeping the company as a viable concern.

His speech was slurred slightly and he was going to have problems with the left side of his body for a long while, but his mind was still alive and sharp.

Suddenly the real reason why Freya had pleaded with him to come home for Christmas was only too apparent. Elstrom Mapping was finished. Over. After two hundred years of creating maps and sea charts, the company was dead in the water.

A dinosaur.

That was the exact word that his father had managed to say to describe the family business that he had devoted his life to. An extinct creature which no longer had a place in the modern world.

His father had given up in every way possible.

How could this have happened so quickly? Two years ago, the business was not only healthy but thriving and he had almost managed to convince his father that modern technology was the best way forward. There had been plans. A budget. They had actually laughed that Elstrom would last another two hundred years.

But, of course, that was before he'd walked out on the company, leaving his stepbrother in charge.

Travis had taken over and destroyed Elstrom Mapping from the inside out. And his father had let it happen without a fight rather than admit that he had made a horrible mistake.

Now he wanted Scott to finish the job that he had started. Would he do it? Would he take over the company and be the final Elstrom at the helm? Even if it was for a short time, it would please him to think that Elstrom Mapping was still in the family.

What choice did he have? Of course he had to say yes.

He loved his sister and admired her more than he could say but there was only one thing that photograph screamed out to him and it had nothing to do with happy memories.

It was failure.

He had failed. Their marriage had failed and Alexa had betrayed him in the worst way possible. The last thing he needed today was a reminder of his past.

Just the opposite. He was going to need every scrap of positive energy he possessed if he had any hope of making good on the promise he had made to his father that afternoon. And a whole lot more.

Nothing was going to stand in his way.

He was going to have to pick up the pieces and prove that he could do what Travis couldn't. Save Elstrom from going to the wall.

Elstrom Mapping was his. And it was not going to fail.

CHAPTER THREE

'So come on. Spill. What happened last night with you and the scruffy rich lumberjack?'

'Nothing happened,' Toni replied with a light casual lilt.

There was a roar of boos and hisses from around the chaos of the breakfast table in the tiny apartment Lucy shared with her flatmates and, for the last few days, her pal Amy Baldoni. Usually it was clean and organised. But this morning there were three girls crammed into the small kitchen diner with all of the kit they needed for their six months gap year expedition parked in the hallway. And they were eating as though it was the last decent breakfast they would have for ages. This was probably not far from the truth.

'Come on, Antonia—' Lucy grinned '—we know that guilty look.'

'Guilty? *Moi?*' Toni replied and pressed her right hand to her bosom in the most elegant ladylike manner.

'Who's guilty?' Amy laughed as she waltzed in with her huge rucksack slung over one shoulder.

'The girls are accusing me of holding out on the tantalising news about Scott Elstrom, that's all,' Toni replied and pressed her lips together tightly.

'Aha. Busted. You are looking remarkably perky for a twenty-seven-year-old lady who partied late into the night,'

Amy replied and set her rucksack in a corner before taking her place at the table, loading her plate with toast and marmalade and ham and cheese croissants. 'Go on, then,' Amy said before biting into the toast. 'Out with it.'

'We did have a small interlude after you all left,' Toni replied in a totally casual voice. 'The man was jet-lagged, ate all the pizza and most of the pan of brownies. And no—' she pointed to Lucy, who was just about to say something rude between eating because she always did '—I did not ask him to warm my toes for me or any other parts.'

'Why not?' Amy asked between chewing. 'You promised that this year was going to be different. Now that creepy Peter is out on his ear, you're young, free and single. All ready for a new date to be installed by the summer. That was what we agreed, wasn't it?'

'Was that at the New Year's party?' Lucy blinked. 'I don't remember much after that third cocktail. Or was it the fifth?'

'New Year resolutions definitely have an expiry date.' Toni laughed then caught the look that Amy was giving her. 'Okay, I did sort of say that this year was going to be the start of new exciting things. New job. Lots more travel. New central heating boiler! Redecorating! Those things can be exciting too. So you can stop booing. A new boyfriend is an optional extra.'

'Six months, darling sister,' Amy replied, pointing her toast at her. 'You said that you would be fixed up in six months. I have an excellent memory for facts and dates!'

'Anyhow, when I surfaced an hour ago his bedroom door was open, his breakfast dishes were washed and draining in the kitchen and the house was in silence. The man had obviously gone to work on a Sunday. Either that or the sight of so many lovely ladies in their lingerie last night was more than he could stand and he took off back to Alaska.'

'Alaska,' Lucy sighed. 'That's on my list.' Then she sniffed. 'But not this trip. Way too cold. Bring on the sun. Oh. Speaking of which. We have twenty minutes until the boys get here.' And with that she slurped her coffee and scraped back her chair.

'Packing. That would be good. Be back soon. Amy, have you seen my hair straighteners?'

Toni got to her feet and started clearing away the breakfast plates as Amy chuckled into her tea and toast.

'Hair straighteners? I think Lucy may be in for a bit of a disappointment when she gets to the campsite.' Amy waved her hand from side to side and rocked her shoulders. 'Apparently the electricity generators can be a bit temperamental.'

Then she looked up at Toni and grinned. 'Don't look so worried. I've packed a tool kit with a full set of screwdrivers into my suitcase. We shall—' and she waved her butter knife in the air '—have power. So fear not, darling sister, the magical sat phone will be charged at regular intervals. How else am I going to be able to keep tabs on this amazing love life you promised to throw yourself into? I can see our house being turned into a real little love nest now that you've cleared out the lodger. Cool!'

Then she tucked into the marmalade with great gusto.

'You are incorrigible!' Toni replied with a grin and flicked the tea towel towards Amy. '*Love nest?* Where did you hear that expression? You know that it's totally going to be the other way around! The boys will be falling over themselves when they take a look at you! Try not to break all of their hearts.'

'Can't promise a thing.' Amy smirked and then startled Toni by wrapping her arms around her and giving her a

big squishy hug. 'I'm going to miss you but you understand why I don't want you at the airport making a mushy
scene, don't you?' Then, before Toni could answer, she
stepped back and dropped her plate and cutlery into the
sink. 'Thanks for doing the washing-up! I should probably get dressed.'

And, with a wide-armed stretch, Amy walked slowly
back to the bedroom where, from the sound of it, Lucy
and two of her flatmates were already arguing about what
to take in their hand luggage.

Madness. Total madness.

But she waited until Amy was out of sight before pulling out a tissue and blowing her nose. *Stupid girl.* She had
known this day was coming since Christmas and she had
promised Amy that she would not get all gooey…but look
at the state that she was in!

Of course she understood. That was why she was here
now instead of weeping buckets at the departure gate. But
it didn't make it any easier.

It helped if she imagined it was Scott Elstrom's face at
the bottom of the washing-up bowl.

This was entirely his fault!

Her brain had been spinning most of the night, working through the options, over and over again, weighing up
the pros and cons, and the more she thought about it, the
more obvious the answer had become.

She had to convince Scott that he should sit for a portrait in place of his father.

He was the new head of the company, after all. It was
his duty to go ahead with the project that Freya had already paid half in advance. Wasn't it?

But there was something else which kept whirling
around inside her head every time she'd punched her
feather pillow to try and find a comfy spot.

Freya had come running to her to ask for help. It had to be a Baldoni. No one else would do!

Surely that had to give her some bargaining power?

Toni scrubbed extra hard on the frying pan. Now all she had to do was pluck up enough courage to insist on it the next time she saw Scott.

Toni's hands closed around the cool edge of the sink and she closed her eyes for a few seconds.

She didn't have any choice. That portrait had to be finished, one way or another.

She needed the rest of the money to pay for Amy's university fees in the autumn.

Girlish laughter broke through her thoughts and Toni smiled as she stacked the cups and plates.

Amy was right.

This *was* her chance to make a new start and claim her life.

The little girl who she'd promised to take care of the morning their parents died was a young woman now with her own life.

Amy was amazing and was going to go far in life. She knew exactly what she wanted and how she was going to get it. It had been Amy's idea to talk to the university professors who were going to be teaching her and find out what kind of expedition would suit the coursework. Thinking ahead. Planning her future.

She had taught her sister well.

They had watched the dawn come up together in the garden of their little family house early on New Year's morning and made promises to one another that could not be broken.

In three months' time both of their lives would be completely different. Amy would be in Peru and working hard. And she would have finished this portrait, cleared out the clutter from their little house and redecorated every room. All ready for their cute London house to be rented out for the next three years while Amy was at university.

This was her chance to take her photography career to the next level and she was ready to grab it with both hands and do what it took to learn from the best. Travel. Live a little. Maybe even find the time to enjoy herself.

It was scary to think of the transformation that was going to take place but it was make the change now or stay locked in the same groove forever.

She chose now.

By the time she was thirty, her plan was to have the Antonia Baldoni photographic studio up and running. No more working for someone else. No more being taken for granted. No more being used by other people.

Three more years' experience and training and she would be ready to start out on her own.

Starting with this portrait.

This was not the time to let one man who refused to have his portrait painted get in the way of Amy's education.

Scott Elstrom was not going to escape that easily. And if she had to become a total pest to make that happen? Then so be it.

Because the new and improved version of Antonia Baldoni had decided to make some changes in her life and it all kicked off today.

Look out, world. Here I come. *Bring it on.*

Scott strode down the busy London pavement in the light morning sleet, wincing in pain.

His senses were assaulted by a cacophony of noise which seemed to come from every direction. Cars, buses, taxi cabs and motorcyclists. And people. So many people all crushed together. Jostling and pushing and manoeuvring around one another.

What were they all doing here at this time on a Sunday morning? Strange. He had forgotten what the barrage of noise and bustle of city life was like. Right now, his life in Alaska seemed like a distant dream. A fantasy of calm and quiet and beauty and…

He jumped out of the way as a cycle courier flashed across the path in front of him at high speed with only inches to spare. The light sleet mixed with loose snow that had been falling most of the night had made the pavements treacherous for cyclists.

Control. In Alaska he was in control of where and what and how he lived his life. The climate and the harsh conditions were all part of the job. He respected that. But here? Here, he had to battle very different challenges.

And every one of them was just as tough as climbing a mountain range or crossing sea ice.

But that was what he was here for.

He had promised his father and sister that he would give the family business six months of his life and stay in London until early September.

Six long and arduous months which right at that moment felt like an eternity of living in the city.

It was Freya who'd filled Scott in on the details when they had taken off to the hospital café to leave their father to rest.

The plan was to sell the building to property developers, who would give them a serious amount of money to build apartments in such a prestigious address. Any remaining charts and maps would be snapped up by collectors and specialist museums. With the money from the sales there would enough to pay off the debts and have some left over for their father's retirement.

Because otherwise? Otherwise, things were going down so fast that it would mean bankruptcy and their father couldn't tolerate the idea of not paying his bills to the suppliers who had been so loyal for the past few years.

Last resort? They had an amazing offer from a marketing company who wanted to create tacky mapping merchandise using the Elstrom company name.

Freya had been quite shocked at his expletive-laden reply to that suggestion and had to ask him to lower his voice.

No way. He was not going to see two hundred years of his family heritage handed over as a prestige symbol on cheap magnifying glasses and plastic rulers.

Little wonder that Freya had telephoned him to ask him to come home. His baby sister certainly knew what buttons to press to bring on even more guilt.

Lars Elstrom had just handed him the keys to the shop. He would be damned if he was going to be the one turning the lights out on the day they closed for good.

But it was more than that and he knew it.

It had been his decision to walk away and leave the company two years ago when things went off the rails in his life. He could have fought his father's decision to appoint Travis to run the company through hard evidence and facts.

Instead, he had forced his father to choose between his apparently charming and talented and inspirational new stepson, Travis, and the angry man who Scott had become.

And that one decision had cost the company.

And now the stepson was long gone, the money had run out and suddenly his father needed him to step in and help the company with as much peace and dignity as he could.

How ironic was that?

But one thing was not so clear. Had he come back in

time to save Elstrom Mapping? Because that was precisely what he intended to do. Or go down trying.

It was going to take all of his strength and ingenuity to survive the next six months.

Just as he had survived when his world was destroyed two years ago. Taking things one day at a time.

Starting right now.

Head back, chin up, Scott stopped outside the antique facade of Elstrom Mapping and glanced up at the old three-storey building which had been his playground and school as a boy, his centre in the middle of his parents' divorce and then his chance to get close to his father again when he came to work here.

It had been two years since he had stood outside this door and waved goodbye to Freya as casually as if he were heading to the pub instead of a series of long arduous flights to a remote environmental survey base in Alaska.

It felt a lot longer.

Freya had organised a very casual meal out for the family before he took off and he had been a bear the whole evening. Bad-tempered and sullen and quiet. He couldn't even recall why. Probably some snide remark his father had made about how much the business needed him to bring some new orders—with Travis managing the company they could use someone experienced to work with clients on operational mapping projects in the field.

Scott could see that now in hindsight but he had been blind to just how overwhelmed his father had been at the time by everything that had happened.

Two stubborn men. As different as possible from one another. It was hard to believe that they were even related.

They were from different planets which only collided in astrological time zones.

Neither of them ready to admit that the other person might need help.

Neither of them willing to talk about the real problem that was never going away.

No way was his father going to lower himself to plead with Scott to give up a paying job and a contract he had signed to come back to London and dig Elstrom out of a large hole which had nothing to do with him and everything to do with his own bad judgement.

Scott clenched his fingers tight around the elaborate key set that Freya had passed him and braced his jaw as he turned the three keys, one after the other.

His feet hesitated for just a fraction of a second before he brushed the fear away.

Time to find out just how bad things had become. Because, for better or worse, he was in charge of Elstrom Mapping now and things were going to have to change. And fast.

Two hours later, Toni stepped down from the red London bus and darted under the shelter of the nearest shop doorway. The February rain had swept in and was pounding on the fabric awning above her head and bouncing off the pavement of the narrow street in this smart part of the city.

Her gaze skipped between the pedestrians scurrying for cover until it settled on the elegant three-storey stone building across the street.

What was she doing here? She was a commercial photographer and wannabe studio business owner.

Toni closed her eyes and wallowed in ten seconds of self-pity and shame before shaking herself out of it. This had been her decision. Nobody had forced her to take Freya Elstrom's offer when she'd called. But Freya had kept going on about how important it was to her father that

a Baldoni had to paint the last of the Elstroms. It meant a
lot to him and he was willing to pay her a special bonus
if she could drop everything and work on the portrait in
the next few months.

Now she knew the reason for the sudden urge to have
his portrait painted was nothing to do with artistic appreciation and a lot more to do with the fact that the poor
man was ill.

The last of the Elstrom family. A shiver ran across Toni's
shoulders. She didn't like the sound of that.

Like it or not, she and Amy were the last of the Baldoni
dynasty. Her father had been an only child and the only
male cousins were far more interested in IT than fine arts.

Perhaps she had more in common with Scott Elstrom
than she was prepared to admit?

Now all she had to do was convince him that the best
thing for the business was to have his portrait painted. She
couldn't return the fee. The money had already been spent
on Amy's round-the-world plane ticket. And she needed
the rest of the fee to help her through university.

So Scott had better get used to the idea.

Being immortalised in oil and acrylics was quite pain-
less really.

Oh, yes. A man who chose to work in Alaska in the
middle of winter was really going to go for that idea.

Now that did give her the shivers. That and the rivulet
of rain water spilling out from the awning.

She was doomed!

Toni dropped her shoulders and shoved her free hand
into the pocket of the practical but not very elegant all-
weather coat she used for outdoor photo shoots.

The things she did for her sister!

Two weeks. She had two weeks' holiday to sketch the

portrait and work in at least two full sittings before heading back to work. She could finish the portrait at home over the next few weekends and collect the rest of her fee. With a bit of luck, there might be a little left over from paying Amy's university fees to squeeze in a quick holiday somewhere warm and sunny.

Now that—she shivered in the icy wind—would be nice.

Exhaling slowly, Toni glanced from side to side to find a gap in the stream of people who had their heads down, their umbrellas braced forward against the driving sleet and rain and oblivious to anyone who might walk in their way.

Seizing on a momentary lull, Toni dashed out onto the road in the stationary rush hour traffic. She had almost made it when she had to dive sideways to dodge a bicycle courier and planted her right foot into a deep puddle. Dirty cold water splashed up into her smart high heeled ankle boots and trickled down inside, making her gasp with shock.

Hissing under her breath, Toni stepped up onto the kerb and inside the porch.

A brass plaque set into the old stone read: 'Elstrom and Sons. Map-makers' in the most stunning cursive script.

Blowing out hard, Toni rolled back her shoulders and tried to think positive thoughts. A flutter of nervous apprehension winged across her stomach.

This was so ridiculous.

She was here to paint Scott's portrait. That was all. The small fact that he did not actually want his portrait painting was not important.

Much. She peered through the tiny squares of thick old glass set into the door but couldn't see a thing—no lights or movement.

She ran her hands down the front of her raincoat and lifted her chin, stretched her hand out and rang the doorbell.

Instantly a low buzzing sound came from the door and a green light flashed.

Oh. Right. Security door. Well, that made sense.

She turned the handle, pushed the door a little and stepped inside.

Water dripping from every part of her, Toni shook the rain from her hair and instantly inhaled the glorious deep, rich aroma of antique wood, polished leather and that certain delicious muskiness that came from old manuscripts and bound books.

Laughing and half choking in the slightly dusty air, a sudden smile caught her unexpectedly.

Strange, Toni thought. That smell. It was so distinctive. She inhaled deeply and instantly recognized it. Of course. Her mother used to have a tin of beeswax and linseed oil mixed with lavender under the sink and brought it out whenever she dusted her father's studio, which wasn't often, considering how rarely any flat surface remained uncluttered with paperwork and art exhibition catalogues and letters and, occasionally, bills.

She hadn't thought about that polish for years. Perhaps she should make some up when she got back to the house to protect the furniture against the ravages of a new tenant?

The door buzzed behind her, demanding to be closed, breaking the spell.

Then she stood, frozen and blinking, trying to take in what she was looking at.

It was like stepping back in time. Light streamed into the space from long, narrow stained glass window panels at the other side of the room that seemed to lead into a corridor. But in front of her, on either side, the walls were covered in rows of square wooden panels probably not wider than her arm above a tough-looking, very weath-ered wooden floor.

No carpet or textiles. Just hardwood panelling.

Cupboards and cabinets were lined up to her left and at head height along each wall were sea charts and maps in heavy gilt frames.

Well, that explained the security door!

The last time she had seen anything like this was at a stately home which had not been touched for hundreds of years. The financial demands of keeping the place going had finally caught up with the family and they had very reluctantly opened their home as a film set for historical dramas. The media company she worked for had been there for months, filming what they needed.

But this room? This was more like a museum.

Toni strolled over to a stunning wide table decorated in marquetry which stretched the full length of one wall. It was covered with scrolls, brightly coloured documents inside plastic sheets and an assortment of what looked, to her uneducated eyes, like antique survey equipment and sextants.

She was so engrossed in admiring the stunning elabo-rate engraving on the handle of a brass magnifying glass that it took a blast of cold air on her neck to snap her back into the real world. Toni whirled around in surprise and inhaled sharply.

Little wonder. A towering dark blond-haired man filled the entrance to the corridor, blocking out the light. He was wearing a navy blue round-necked light sweater with the sleeves rolled up, oblivious to the cold and wet outside.

His deeply tanned face was glowing from the rain and wind and he ran the fingers of his right hand back through his long damp hair from forehead to neck in a single natural motion. That simple movement only made his paler heavy eyebrows and pepper-and-salt moustache and beard even more pronounced.

Last night at the town house, his eyes had seemed dark and cloudy. But here Toni realised just how wrong she had been.

Despite the lack of a comfortable bed, the exhaustion had faded to a slight crease between those eyebrows, drawing her gaze to eyes the colour of a Mediterranean sea.

His square jaw was so taut it might have been sculpted. But it was his mouth that knocked the air out of her lungs, and had her clinging on to the edge of the table for support.

Plump lips smiled wide above his light beard, so that the bow was sharp between the smile lines.

His button-fly denims sat low on his slim hips but there was no mistaking that he was pure muscle beneath those tight trousers. Because, as he stood there for a second, his hands thrust deep into his trouser pockets, looking from table to table, scanning the horizon that was the confines of the shop, every movement he made seemed magnified.

The entire room seemed to shrink around him.

How did he do that? How did he just waltz in and master the room as though he was in command of the space and everyone in it?

This man was outdoors taken to the next level. No wonder he worked in Alaska. She could certainly imagine him standing at the helm of some ice-breaker, head high, legs braced. The master of his universe.

The hair on the back of her neck prickled with recognition.

Instead of giving her the up and down once-over, his gaze locked on to her face and stayed there, unmoving for a few seconds, before the corner of his mouth slid into a lazy smile.

The corners of those amazing eyes crinkled slightly and the warmth of that smile seemed to heat the air between them. And, at that moment, this smile was for her. And her heart leapt. More than a little. But just enough to recognize that the blush of heat racing through her neck and face were not due to the extra-warm coat and scarf that she was wearing.

In that instant Toni knew what it felt like to be the most important and most beautiful person in the room. Heart thumping. Brain spinning. An odd and unfamiliar tension hummed down her veins. Every cell of her suddenly alive and tuned into the vibrations emanating from his body.

Suddenly she wanted to preen and flick her hair and roll her shoulders back so that she could stick her chest out.

It was as if she had been dusted with instant lust powder.

Standing a little straighter, Toni quickly focused her gaze on the engraving on the glass that she was still holding, trying to find something to do with her hands, only too aware that he was still watching her.

She could practically feel the heat of that laser beam gaze burning a hole through her forehead and was surprised that there was no smell of smoke or a scorch mark on the wall behind her.

'Miss Baldoni. I'm surprised to see you here at this time on a Sunday morning. I thought that you might be enjoying a lie-in. I do hope that I didn't wake you up on my way out this morning. It was very early.'

'I didn't hear a thing, Mr Elstrom. As for my being here?' Toni very carefully put down the glass and lifted her chin. 'As I explained last night, I have a contract to paint the head of Elstrom Mapping. No matter whom that may be.' She braved a small smile. 'I am so looking forward to painting your portrait. Perhaps we can get started with some photographs? Show me your best pose. I dare you!'

CHAPTER FOUR

SCOTT'S REPLY WAS to rest his hands, splayed out, on the table, his left hand loose and relaxed, the right bandaged around the fingers. He leaned the top half of his long wide frame towards her from the hips so that she had to fight the urge to lean back against the display table and protect her space.

She liked hands, always had. It was usually one of the first things she noticed about a person. She could tell from the way he protected his bandaged fingers that he must be in pain. His left hand had long slender fingers with clean short nails. The knuckles were scarred and bruised as though they had been bashed at regular intervals and the veins on the back of his hand stood out in prominent raised rivers. Sinewy. Powerful.

They were clever, fast, working hands.

No manicures for Scott Elstrom.

The neck of his top stretched open and revealed a hint of deeply tanned skin around the neckline and more than a few dark blond chest hairs.

At this distance, she could have reached out and touched the curved flicks of thick blond slicked-back hair that had fallen over one side of his temple, but she had the idea that he would like that far too much so she simply lifted her chin and inhaled a long calming breath through her nose.

Big mistake.

Instead of a background aroma of leather and lavender and old books, she was overwhelmed with the scent of gentle rain on freshly cut grass blended with lime zest which was tangy and fresh against the sweetness of the air.

He had certainly made good use of the bath at Freya's!

He smelt wonderful. Expensive, distinctive and on a scale of one to ten on the testosterone level she would give him a twelve. From the sun-bleached hair on his arms and the way the muscles in his neck flexed when he moved, to the know-it-all confidence in the smile he was giving her at that moment, he was off the scale.

He was about as different from Peter as it was possible to be—on the surface.

He was a fashion photographer's dream. She knew several professionals who would have signed him on the spot if they had seen him like this. And somehow she had to paint his portrait! Wow! *Thank you, Freya.*

So what if she was attracted to him? It was only natural.

Until now, she had believed that she was immune to such charms. After all, she had been exposed to this type of infection many times before and just about survived. Working in studio photography exposed her to egos the size of small planets most days of the week, girls and boys.

But this man was a carrier for a super-powerful version of charm that no amount of previous experience had a chance of fighting off.

For a moment her heart went out to him.

He had travelled thousands of miles to come back to take over a family business with frostbitten fingers. The last thing he needed was a pest like her turning up to annoy him.

Then his gaze shot to her face. It was fierce and intense, and for one microsecond she had an insight into the power and strength of this man who could freeze her to ice with just one glance.

She might have guessed. He probably expected everyone to jump when he clicked his fingers and not complain in the process.

'There seems to be a misunderstanding, Miss Baldoni. I thought that I made it clear last night that the situation has changed. And I have no plans to have my portrait painted by you or anyone else for that matter.'

His voice came from the depths of his chest and was no doubt intended to intimidate lesser mortals who got in his way.

Not this time! She was way too used to dealing with the divas of the media world to let a feeble excuse like logic stop her from getting her way.

She needed this commission!

'Oh, I understand what you're telling me perfectly, Mr Elstrom. Plans do have a nasty habit of changing on us without warning, don't they? It's most inconvenient.'

Rubbing her hands together in delight, Toni dived into her capacious shoulder bag and pulled out her digital camera. 'My motto? Let's look at this as an opportunity. In fact, I was just telling Freya this morning that I have a wonderful feeling that this project is going to be something extra special.'

His nose wrinkled and a sound close to a low, deep grunt escaped his lips. 'You spoke to Freya?'

'Well, of course I had to clarify my position. Seeing as she has already paid me half my fee. And guess what? Your father is *so* looking forward to seeing your final portrait! He can hardly wait to see it join the others in your boardroom.'

Then she grinned, fluttered her eyelashes at him, raised

the camera to her eyes and fired off a flash photograph of his stunned face before he could say a word.

'Excellent. Now, shall we peek at the gallery?'

'The gallery?' he asked with a less than happy expression on his face, eyebrows high.

'The Baldoni collection, of course. I would love to see my father's work again. And you can talk to me about the Elstrom family history at the same time. What fun!'

His lips formed the word 'fun'—at least she thought that the word was fun—and he made that low groaning sound again.

'Only if you promise not to even try to take my photograph again.'

'No photographs? That's going to make it tricky.'

'Camera-shy,' he murmured.

'Okay—' she winced '—that's a first but I can handle that. It will mean more work but I can run a few sketches and make notes on your ideas.'

'No ideas. You're on your own, Miss Baldoni. But if you want to see the other portraits before you go, the boardroom is on the first floor.' He nodded to the narrow polished wooden staircase at the other end of the reception area. 'After you.'

'What a wonderful table,' Toni said as she strolled into a long narrow room with wood-panelled walls which was dominated by a stunning table which ran almost the full length of the room. The surface of the table was decorated by inlaid pictures crafted from fine marquetry and gold bands which had been inserted into the golden wood.

She ran her fingers along the wood, which was worn down by wear and slightly rough under her fingertips, and then strolled over to the four large windows which ran from waist to head height. 'Is this stained glass original?'

'The whole building was bomb-damaged during the war so some of the glass was replaced with replicas.'

'It's lovely work.'

Then, with one deep breath, she swung around and, with her back to the windows, plunged her hands deep into the pockets of her coat to try and get some warmth.

Facing her was a collection of some of the most stunning and unusual portraits that she had ever seen.

Looking from left to right, it was immediately clear that the oldest full length paintings were on the wall directly facing the chair at the head of the table. She dashed across the room so that she could take a closer look, moving from picture to picture, nodding and smiling in appreciation of the remarkable workmanship. And chatting to herself as she went.

'Now that older gent with the sea charts and sextant—that has to be of the seafaring Elstrom shipping clan. All beards and rough and tough dangerous sea crossings. But this one.' She paused and tapped her lower lip and tilted her head to one side. 'This Elstrom looks more studious. Was he a scientist?'

She turned around to ask Scott but he was standing at the other end of the room, close to the door, with his gaze totally focused on the centre of the table. Deep in thought and totally oblivious to her and what she had been asking.

Toni had staged photo shoots long enough to recognize that something was very wrong with the man she was looking at.

His shoulders were braced hard, his jaw was locked tight shut and those eyes were not blue at all but had turned as grey and steely as the ocean waves on the portraits she had just been looking at. Dark. Stormy. And troubled.

Everything about Scott's body language screamed out to her that he took absolutely no pleasure in being in this room.

Well, that made sense. The last twenty-four hours must have been quite a roller coaster. His father was ill and he'd had a terrible journey from Alaska to take over a job when he wasn't expecting it. She would be totally wrecked! Maybe she should be a little more forgiving? Her journey this morning had been a short ride on a heated bus.

She quickly glanced away and pretended to move to the next portrait and then the next until she came to an Elstrom in a business suit and a painting style that was totally familiar to her. Instinct and a slight rustle of papers behind her back told her that Scott had moved.

'Ah. Look at that classic pose,' she called out in a cheery voice. 'Your grandfather must have been a wonderful chairman of the board. So dominant. My grandfather really did capture something about him. There is real spirit behind those eyes.'

Toni glanced across at Scott but he seemed more interested in scanning through a bundle of mail he had brought with him from the reception area.

'But we can be more creative if you want,' she suggested and stepped closer to him. 'Maybe even take it out of doors and have more of an action shot. Sailing could work. Or mountaineering? Just pass me some action shots and let me work my magic. All good control metaphors.'

'Control metaphors,' he repeated. 'That sounds good. Do you do this a lot?'

Suddenly Toni's patience ran out. 'My CV is with Freya and your father sounded very keen on me painting something worthy of hanging on these walls next to your family. Is there a problem I don't know about here? Or is the problem with me? Because, for the record, I don't normally spend my evenings modelling lingerie.'

That got his attention and the mail hit the table.

'For the record. My decision to cancel your contract

has nothing to do with what happened last night. You have every right to hold a birthday party if you choose.'

'Cancel? Oh, no...' She coughed and shook her head. 'Freya told me that this was a top priority job. I turned work away to come here to do this. You don't cancel at this short notice. I won't allow it.'

Then she whirled around and waved her arm towards the paintings.

'This is your family! My grandfather started the tradition of painting portraits of every head of the Elstroms, starting with your great-grandfather right down to that one of your uncle, which my dad worked on when I was a girl. And now it's my turn. Tradition. I like that idea just fine. You are carrying on the family tradition and so am I. So you're having your portrait painted whether you like it or not.'

She blinked and grinned but his reaction was to close his eyes for a second and cross his arms.

'Then let me explain again. It's very simple. I have absolutely no intention of having a painting of my face hanging on that wall and I certainly do not have the time to sit around while you sketch my wrinkles. As far as I'm concerned, you can take your fee and go home right now. Think of it as a bonus.'

'Are you serious?' she choked. 'You dragged me all the way out here to the centre of London to do the work and now you've changed your mind? Is that what you're telling me?'

'I haven't changed my mind. This was never my idea in the first place. The first thing I knew about it was when you told me last night. My sister made the arrangements, not me.'

'I have a signed contract,' Toni replied, crossing her arms to match his, her eyebrows high.

'I can cancel it and you can keep your fee. Go home with my blessing.'

'Just like that?' she gasped.

'Just like that. You will have your fee in the bank today. I'm sorry for wasting your time. Do we have a deal, Miss Baldoni?'

He held out his hand and she took it. And held it and kept on holding it until he looked down and frowned and tried to pull it away.

'What are you doing?'

'My job. Part of creating a portrait is making a connection with the sitter so you can capture something unique about them. I always start with the hands. Or, in your case, one hand. I like hands and yours is spectacular.'

She gave a quick nod. 'You like being outdoors and working for a living in hard environments. Alaska makes sense now. Yes. I can do something with that. And it explains why you're so grumpy here in the office.'

'I am not grumpy,' he said and pulled his hand back. 'Did you hear what I said? You're going to have your fee. So feel free to go and do one of those jobs that you passed over to come here.'

'Grumpy. Here is how it works. I sign a contract and I deliver the goods. No arguments, no discussion; that is what's going to happen.'

He glared at her and did the eyebrow thing again. 'Are you always so stubborn?'

'Frequently. Especially with uncooperative subjects like you. So you may as well get used to the idea, because I am painting you. Even if I have to do it from memory and press clippings. That's the way it works.'

She stepped back and made a square with the thumb and forefingers of both hands. 'Oh. Would you mind doing that look again? Scowl a little more to one side. That's super. I was looking for a scary image for Halloween.'

'Double the fee if you leave now.'

That stopped her and she clasped hold of one of the boardroom's carved wooden chairs.

'What? No. I gave Freya my word that I would do the very best work that I could. Promises mean something in my family. If I give my word that I will do something I will do it. End of story.'

'Is it? Let me guess. I know a few things about families too. Something tells me that you're desperate to prove to your father, the famous portrait painter, that you're his equal.'

He leant back against the wooden panels with a smug expression on his face. 'Am I right?'

The words hit Toni like a slap across the face and she reeled back in a reflex action which had her gasping for breath.

Suddenly it all became too much. Lack of sleep, the sadness of waving Amy goodbye as she drove away in a taxi, and then the harshness of this man all combined together in one mighty wave which washed over her, leaving her exhausted.

Toni whirled around sideways to look at the portrait that her father had painted. There was no way that she was going to let Scott see how close she was to bursting into tears.

It was several minutes before she was ready to reply in a hoarse whisper. 'Whose family are we talking about? Yours or mine? Because I'm sorry to disappoint you, Mr Elstrom, but this time you're wrong. My father passed away several years ago. The only person I have to prove anything to is myself.'

There was a sharp intake of breath followed by a long slow sigh. 'My apologies. I didn't know.'

Toni replied with a sharp nod. 'There is no reason why you should know. But, you see, I really am the last of the Baldoni artists and your father wants a Baldoni hanging on this wall. Which means. Me.'

Toni half turned from the waist and risked glancing at Scott, who was looking at her with something close to respect in his eyes.

She stood in silence for a moment and then her shoulders dropped. 'Freya has already paid me half my fee for the portrait. I don't want to give that money back.' Then she shrugged. 'In fact I have already spent it on something important—but that doesn't matter.'

She lifted her chin but carried on in a softer voice. 'What does matter is that I want to deliver this portrait. I can work on your likeness from photos and sketches. But it makes a big difference if I can get my client to sit down and be fairly still for a while. I can see that might be a problem. So tell me how we can work together to make this happen.'

Scott waved an arm around in a circle.

'I cannot give you that time. Look around you, Miss Baldoni. I have just been made the head of a company which no longer exists. My father decided to close the business a month ago and make the few remaining staff redundant.'

His fingers clasped around the back rung of a chair.

'It's going to take me months to sort out the financial situation and come up with some sort of rescue package before this building is sold to developers. Apparently, they could make at least six luxury apartments out of this three-storey building.'

'Apartments? Oh, no. That's terrible. Are they allowed to do that? Seriously?'

'Oh, yes. Specialist builders can prop up the creaky outside walls and make the structure safe and strong but it will mean gutting the inside and starting again. Two hundred years of history is about to be wiped away as if it never happened.'

'I see. Well, that explains something I'd been wondering about,' Toni replied in a low voice, almost mumbling to herself before she looked up into Scott's face to find him looking quizzically at her.

'From what Freya told me, your father has been working here most of his life and took over about twenty years ago—that must be from your uncle. Yes? But he didn't have his portrait painted. Even though he is obviously very traditional. It makes sense now. This was going to be his last chance to be painted as the head of Elstrom Mapping before the company closed. He wanted the last portrait on the wall on the day the building was sold.'

She pushed her hands deep into her pockets. 'That's sad,' she sniffed.

'Sad but true. Because you're right.'

He stepped in front of the portrait painted by Toni's father and they stood side by side and stared up at the young, vibrant blond-haired man whose essence had been captured in oil paint on canvas.

'My uncle Neil was the action businessman—the dynamic and charming star who was a natural athlete and medal-winning explorer. He excelled in public speaking, making presentations and was dazzling to the media. While my father…?'

Scott pushed his hands into his trouser pockets.

'My father worked out as a boy that he was never going to compete with his older brother Neil. He preferred to stay in the background and let his brother take the lime-light. So they sat down and worked it out between them. My father would stay here in the office and do the meticulous work behind the scenes while my uncle Neil travelled the world using Elstrom maps and bringing in more orders than they could cope with. It was win/win. Until my uncle was killed in an avalanche in the Himalayas. And the whole thing fell apart.'

'Now it's my turn to be sorry. He looks like a remarkable man.'

'He was extraordinary. And that was part of the problem. Do you know why my father never contacted the Baldoni family? Because he never once felt that he was the man in charge. I was about twelve when my uncle had the accident and as far as my dad was concerned I was the man who was destined to take my uncle's place. My uncle had never married or settled down anywhere long enough to have a family, although he was never short of female company. Which meant one thing. I was the heir. The man who was going to be the next head of Elstrom Mapping. My father told me on my eighteenth birthday that all he'd been doing was keeping my seat warm for me.'

'Wait. Are you telling me that he never wanted his portrait painted?'

'Never. It was going to be my portrait hanging on the wall next to my uncle. Not my dad. Me.'

'Wow. So why…?'

'He finally accepted this Christmas that it was never going to happen.'

'I don't understand.'

'Oh, it's quite simple. I walked out of this building two years ago and made it perfectly clear that I had absolutely no intention of ever coming back. That was it. Unless Freya suddenly developed a burning fascination for

sea charts, the Elstrom line ended with my dad. I was out
and was out for good.'

Scott nodded to the wall and as he spoke every word
seemed to come from a deep, dark place. 'It has taken
two years for him to finally get that fact into his head and
admit defeat. Lars Elstrom truly would be the last head
of Elstrom Mapping. There was no way he was going to
get me to come back and run the business. No way at all.'

Then he turned around to face her and leant back
against the table. Head high. Eyes narrow and all business.

'Do you get the picture now, Miss Baldoni?'

CHAPTER FIVE

TONI SAT BACK in one of the boardroom chairs and tried to take in what Scott had just told her.

Scott Elstrom didn't want to be here one little bit. In fact he had made it clear to his family that he had no intention of ever coming back to run the business.

No wonder he was grumpy!

She knew what it was like to be dragged out of your normal life by a situation out of your control.

When her parents died in the train crash she had been left utterly alone at eighteen with a ten-year-old sister to bring up.

Scott was lucky. He still had his parents and a sister who cared about him. He could pull this off. *If he wanted to.*

'But you're back to stay now. Aren't you?' she asked cautiously.

'I promised my father that I would give him six months.' Scott's voice was flat and cold but at least he had stopped scowling at her.

Toni pushed off from the chair and flipped both hands into the air with a big grin on her face.

'Then everything has changed. Your face should be right up here on this wall next to your uncle. Six weeks or six months—it doesn't make the slightest bit of difference to me. You're the latest CEO of Elstrom Mapping and it's my job to paint your portrait.'

Then she rubbed her hands together. 'Any chance of a coffee before we get started on the sketches? It's a bit nippy in here.'

Scott didn't move an inch. 'You really aren't going to let this go, are you?'

'Nope—' she grinned '—I have every intention of sticking around and taking your photograph and generally making a nuisance of myself until I have all the material I need to work my magic. It's so important to get to know the client as much as possible. So, you see, there is no way that you're going to get rid of me.'

He stepped forward, totally invading her space until she could see every hair of his grey and blond beard and practically feel his breath on her cheeks.

His skin was red and chapped and his hair needed cutting but somehow Scott Elstrom rocked that master-of-all-he-surveyed look better than any stylist she knew could have pulled off.

Any lesser mortal would have backed off. *Not her.*

'I could pick you up one-handed and carry you outside. You know that, don't you?'

'Absolutely.' She smiled, reached out with her right hand and squeezed his rock-hard biceps, sighing in appreciation, and then her gaze locked on to his eyes. 'But then I would have to set up my paints on the pavement outside your front door and call on all of my media friends to interview me. Just think of the TV crews and reporters who would be hassling you day and night. Wouldn't that be a nice treat?'

'Stalker,' he replied in a low, deep voice which seemed to echo around inside her head and come out of her ears.

'Grumpy.' She blinked then instantly refocused on those startling blue eyes which seemed locked onto hers.

Time expanded. All she could hear was the sound of their breathing and the chiming of a very old clock somewhere in the building.

Oh. And the burning of the air between them as if it was ignited by the fierce electricity that sparked in the few inches that separated them.

She had heard that ozone was addictive and maybe they were right because the air she was breathing now was so thick with pheromones and testosterone she could have sliced it and served it with tea.

It was almost a relief when Scott stepped back. But, to her astonishment, he grabbed her hand with his long strong fingers and started marching towards the door.

Was this it? Was he calling her bluff and throwing her out on to the street?

'Come with me,' he growled. 'I want you to see for yourself why there is no time to spend hours of my life sitting for a portrait.'

It was an office of sorts. But it was totally unlike anywhere she had ever seen.

Every flat or even vaguely flat surface was covered with stacks of paper. All sizes—plain, decorated, scraps of what looked like paper napkins covered in handwriting, envelopes of every description.

Tables, chairs and bookcases were all crammed full of sheets of yellowing paper with the overspill stacked in vague piles on a faded threadbare carpet.

There was a rounded shape in front of the window which might be a sofa because she could see curved wooden feet at either end but, instead of cushions, there were scrolls tied with string and ribbon, about twenty cardboard tubes standing on end and box after box of padded envelopes with exotic bright stamps on the outside.

Floor-to-ceiling bookcases with glass doors lined each wall and Toni could just see through the thick layers of dust that they were crammed to bursting with double-stacked papers and books of all sizes and bindings.

At some point a stack of thin booklets had been knocked off the desk and lay scattered on the floor where they could easily be stepped on.

Scott released her hand with a flick and Toni gingerly stepped forward and picked up one of the booklets.

It was a catalogue promoting *Elstrom Rare Documents Restoration Services*, dated 1958. The original cover must have been a deep blood-red but the colour had faded until it was a faint spotty pink. The letters were blurred and indistinct, the paper inside yellow and fragile.

Replacing the booklet on top of another like it on the desk, Toni looked around at the chaos and swallowed down a lump of cold concern.

'Have you been burgled?'

'Burgled? No.' He laughed. 'This is my dad's private office. Sorry. *Was* my dad's office. Mine now. And it has been like this ever since I can remember.'

'You're kidding me. Seriously? He ran the company from this room?'

'He knows where everything is. Every invoice, every receipt, and every letter he has ever written or received is in this room. You're looking at forty years of his accumulated paperwork plus everything he inherited from my uncle, who had this office before he did.'

'Wow. It's really quite remarkable. Do you mind if I take some photographs?'

'Of what?'

'This room. I had no idea that places like this exist any more.'

'They don't—' he coughed '—not if they want to run as a business. Somewhere in that heap of unopened mail are bills which need to be paid so that the telephones and lights still work. Somewhere. I've been here two hours and I've hardly touched the surface.'

Toni whistled out loud as she took several pictures with her digital camera.

'Good luck with that little challenge.'

Then she snuggled deeper inside her padded coat and looked from side to side. 'I wouldn't even know where to start,' she whispered. 'And this office is freezing; any chance you could turn the heating on—' she cupped her hands and rubbed her palms together '—or is that bad for the documents?'

'Leather and paper like the humidity. It keeps them soft. As for the heating? The temperature seems fine to me, but I haven't had time to check the boiler and the electrics. A building this old has its quirks.'

Toni peeked around Scott and nodded towards the desk.

'How can you not feel cold? I'm standing here shivering.'

He frowned. 'Your hand did feel cool.'

'It's a cold day. By London standards, anyway. Is there a tea room? Kettle? Cups? Anything?'

'Yes. But here's a suggestion.'

Scott grabbed a light padded jacket from the back of a chair stacked with unopened packages. 'Before I set out on a survey I always check that I have the equipment and essential supplies that I need. Food and drink are up there on the top five. As it happens, there are a few things about the city that I do miss when I'm working in the field.'

'Soap and hot water?'

'No. Although those things can be few and far between. But right now I was thinking about real coffee made from ground coffee beans. And something laden with fat and sugar to help me get through this jet lag.'

'Well, I know the local terrain fairly well. Willing to risk having a local guide?'

'Let's get out of here.'

'Two-shot Americano,' they both said at the same time as the barista took their order and then jumped back at the sound of each other's voice.

'Seriously?' He turned and peered at her, arms folded. 'I would have thought that some elegant green tea would be a more suitable hot beverage for a portrait painter. All elegance and refinement and artistic expression.'

Toni snorted out loud. 'Ah, you're back to the stereotypes again. I think it's my solemn duty to flip that illusion and pronto.'

She pressed her right forefinger to her chest. 'A two shot Americano is perfect for a part-time portrait painter who has a day job as a commercial photographer. You get the instant hit from the caffeine but it's not quite enough to bring on a bad case of the jitters. And, believe me, there are some days I'm run so ragged that one coffee has to keep me going for a long time.'

'Aha. So you don't paint portraits full-time. Interesting. Well, that explains a few things.'

'Really. Such as? Please carry on. I would hate for you to keep all of that valuable insight to yourself. What gave the game away?'

To her astonishment, Scott reached across the table and picked up her hand and looked at it, fascinated. Then turned it over and brought it up to his lips.

That simple movement was bad enough, but Toni wasn't

prepared for the rush of heat she got from the touch of his full lips on the sensitive skin at the centre of her palm which had nothing to do with the fact that she had chosen a table right next to the radiator.

It was so unexpected that she took a second before reflex action kicked in and she tried to slide her hand back. No luck. It was locked solidly in his grip of iron.

'What are you doing?' she muttered between locked teeth. 'Stop that right now. People. Are. Looking. At us.'

She smiled over to a group of girls who were giggling at her on another table while she tried to tug her hand away without making it look too obvious.

'Answering your question. So stop struggling. You see, I like hands too. And yours tell me so much about you. No paint under the fingernails or ink or charcoal ground into your palms.'

He pressed his lips to her knuckles and then lowered her hand to the table. 'Your skin smells of shower gel. Not linseed oil or acrylics and it is certainly not used to outside work. A studio photographer. Now, that makes sense.'

'How very observant. I like to think I am creating portraits of a different sort. But—' she took a sip of the scalding-hot fragrant coffee '—you have a point. My first sketches can be taken from a photograph rather than a live sitting straight onto the canvas. That's the way I work. I think about how I want the sitter to look in the final piece. Not always easy.'

He coughed just once and picked up his drink when one of the waitresses nudged him accidentally and the hot coffee splashed on to his bandaged hand, which was resting on the table.

'I'm so sorry. Are you okay?'

'No harm done,' Scott reassured the young girl.

Toni waited until she was gone before looking up at

Scott over the top of her cup. 'Do you mind if I ask—how did you hurt yourself?'

'For a girl, of course! Why else would a man throw himself on to frozen sea ice and let his fingers go anywhere near ice water?'

'Wow. Sea ice. That's astonishing. Scary. Wild. And a bit mad'.

'It's my life. And Dallas does have the most amazing blue eyes.'

'Well, she must have to make you go to those sorts of lengths. Is she okay now? Your Dallas?'

'My Dallas is having the time of her life being pampered and well fed by a whole survey team of boys. Probably not missing me one bit.'

'Not missing you? After what you did for her! That's a bit ungrateful.'

'Probably. Doesn't stop me from missing her. She's been a good friend.'

'Well, in that case the lady is forgiven. Good friends are hard to find. And I hope you finish your business here soon so that you can get back to her charms.'

'I'll drink to that. To Dallas. See you in six months, girl.'

Six months. *Interesting.*

Toni lifted her cup of steaming coffee. 'Six months—is that how long you have to turn the business around?'

'Less. That's how long I have committed to. Different thing.'

'Any ideas about what you're going to do?' Toni asked over the top of her coffee. 'I mean, apart from finding a new office to work from. Because, I have to tell you, I did not see any sign of modern technology just now and I think you might need a few more things besides paper and pens.'

'Maybe. I'm a scientist. And don't look at me like that.

It might be hard to believe. But it's true. Before I make a decision I like to know the facts.'

Scott put down his coffee and nodded back towards the Elstrom building, just down the street. When he spoke it sounded to Toni as though he was simply speaking his thoughts out loud rather than having a conversation. 'Top of the list is to create some operating income. If things are as bad as Freya thinks they are, it could be a shock at the bank tomorrow. Right now, I have no clue about what has happened to our archive of valuable documents— instruments, maps, sea charts going back almost two hundred years. There has to be something left.'

He shrugged and took a long drink before going on. 'I need to make an inventory of the entire stock. Once I know what we have left, I can start work. Sell some items to specialist dealers. Loan others to museums for a fee. That should give me enough time to put together a long-term plan. But I need to work fast. Clear the office. Make space to work. Then I need to create a brilliant sales catalogue in weeks, not months, and...'

Scott's voice faded away and his eyes narrowed and focused on Toni so intently that she glanced around the room before putting her coffee down.

'What? What have I done now?'

'It's not what you *have* done, Miss Baldoni. It's what you are *going* to do.'

He stretched both arms flat on the small table and leant forwards from the waist until he was close enough for her to touch him. 'I need someone who can photograph my stock and create a sales catalogue. Someone with experience as a studio photographer would be absolutely perfect. What do you say?'

Toni gulped down some coffee so fast that she almost choked.

'What do I say?' she replied, blinking. 'I say that Freya paid me to paint your portrait, not work as your commercial photographer.'

Scott slid backwards but his attention was still completely focused on her.

'You wanted to stick around and make character studies. I'm giving you the chance to do that. For the next seven days you can photograph anything you like, including me. On one condition. You help me out with the business side at the same time. Do we have a deal?'

He stretched out his hand across the table and tilted his head slightly to one side.

Toni took a breath, her heart pounding and her mind racing.

Seven days? He was offering her seven days to take the photographs and make the sketches she needed to paint him. And something else. Something even more important. The chance to get to know him a little more.

It was the one thing that had been drummed into her from the very start of her training with her father. To be a real painter, she had to capture the essence of the sitter in paint on the canvas. That was the extra-special quality of a Baldoni portrait. Without that? She might as well just take his photograph and be done with it.

Scott coughed low in his throat and she looked up into eyes which she knew she could paint in a heartbeat. But the rest of him? Somehow, she got the feeling that she had only just touched the surface of the real Scott Elstrom.

So why was she hesitating?

A muscle twitched at the corner of his mouth and her heart rate sped up just enough to answer that question perfectly.

She had known Scott less than a day and she was already far more attracted to him than she had any right to be.

The last time she had worked alone with an attractive man on a project had been the few weeks she'd spent on assignment with Peter. She had fallen and fallen fast and look how well that had turned out. He had lied to her, betrayed her and broken her heart.

Could she trust herself to be more careful with Scott? *But what choice did she have?* She needed this work.

Toni looked into his face, then at his hand, and then back to his face again before sighing out loud and placing her hand in his. It was like being crushed in a vice.

'Fingers! I need the fingers!'

Shaking the blood back into her crushed fingers, she exhaled slowly. 'Well, Mr Scott Elstrom. What have I just let myself in for?'

His reply was an evil chuckle that would have been perfect for a horror movie. 'You saw my dad's office, Antonia. Wait until you see the archive. The Elstrom family take hoarding very seriously.'

A shudder ran across Toni's shoulders. More hoarding! Oh, no. She was an expert on the topic. She had a whole house of her own clutter to clear.

'Come on, girl. Let's make this happen. And on the way I want to hear how you plan to make those dusty old maps of mine look a million dollars. Shall we?'

And with one tiny nod he stepped back and gestured towards the exit. She peered at it for a fraction of a second before rolling her eyes and waving towards the counter. 'Could we have the same again, please? And make that four jam doughnuts this time. I think I'm going to need them.'

CHAPTER SIX

IT WAS ALMOST eight on the Sunday evening when Scott eventually turned the key and staggered into the hallway of Freya's house.

What a day! He would cheerfully take a hard day in the field any time compared to the chaos that was Elstrom Mapping.

The financial situation was not just bad—it was shocking.

His father really had given up. It was obvious from the few decent bank records that he had managed to find, that several valuable items had already been sold to specialist museums so that the loyal skilled staff could have the generous redundancy packages that they deserved.

Damn right. The small team at Elstrom had been the best in the business. Most of them were well beyond retirement age and simply loved working in the old place. The others had been given excellent references and were already working elsewhere.

But the really shocking thing was that all of this had happened over the autumn. A quick call to Freya confirmed what he had started to suspect. That piece of silvery tinsel paper he'd found in one of the drawers was a souvenir from the very last Christmas party that Elstrom would ever hold.

It was enough to bring tears to his eyes. They had always been such amazing parties. Everyone, from corporate clients to solo adventurers and oil exploration companies, would usually be in London for Christmas and found the time to come to Elstrom Mapping to raise a glass.

It was shocking to think that he had missed such a momentous event. And, more than sad, it was tragic to imagine his father sitting in that chair on New Year's Day. Alone. In the wreckage of the business he seemed to have given up on.

That was some start to the New Year.

The only bright spark in his day had been Antonia Baldoni. The girl who had started off as just another nuisance had turned out to be the most astonishing office manager that he had ever met. Not that he was an expert in the subject, but she had worked wonders.

He had been totally sceptical when Antonia suggested clearing one heap of papers at a time and sorting them by date and subject. What difference could it make?

How wrong could he be? In a few hours that bustling brunette bundle of energy and purpose had cleared everything from the huge partners' desk using a battered old tea tray she'd found in the kitchen, giving him space to work.

He had peeked into the boardroom when his back became too stiff to sit any longer and found her sorting every sheet into neat stacks on the boardroom table. And the stacks made sense! She had even found some empty boxes and loaded up the old brochures and pamphlets in case he wanted them for inspiration about future projects.

A single in tray from one of the mapping rooms held everything that needed attention and all of the unopened mail.

He had taken one look at the pile and the fact that Antonia was wearing her hat, coat and gloves to work in and

decided that his first executive decision was to try and get
the heating working in at least the first floor of the building before she froze.

It had taken him almost an hour to coax the ancient gas
boiler down in the freezing dark basement back into life.
At least that hadn't changed. It was as temperamental as
ever and the tangle of electrical wiring looked as though
a toddler had been at play but he could be as stubborn as
Antonia when he wanted to be. Any gas engineer would
probably condemn the old kit, but right now? That was
what they had to work with. And by six she had taken
off her hat and coat. So he had achieved something positive today. Maybe tomorrow she could work without the
gloves?

Good news was in short supply. He would take what
he could.

Starting with Antonia Baldoni.

Apparently he hadn't noticed how messy the house was
that morning when he'd left but there was a lot of clearing
up still to be done after her birthday party. So she had left
the office earlier to tidy up the house.

Scott strolled into the kitchen and turned on the kettle.
He could smell something delicious and savoury cooking
in the oven and the room felt warm and cosy. Hanging up
his coat, he lifted one arm and then the other towards the
ceiling, wincing as the tense muscles complained.

Nothing that about ten hours of decent sleep wouldn't
fix.

Yeah. Like that was going to happen. *Not in that bedroom.* Too many memories. The ghost of his ex-wife was
right there every time he'd woken from a restless dream
of falling through the ice. He didn't need a photograph to
bring back her beautiful face. Just walking into that boardroom at Elstrom had been traumatic enough.

How could he tell Antonia that his last memory of that room had been finding his wife having sex with his stepbrother on the boardroom table?

Not something a man forgot in a hurry. And definitely not an image he was going to share any time soon.

He closed his eyes for a second then blinked awake.

Get over it.

There was no sign of Antonia so he slowly dragged his weary body up the stairs and had only taken a few steps towards his room when the door to the large family bathroom opened.

And through a cloud of hot fragrant steam a small figure emerged.

Antonia was wrapped in a white bath towel which was just large enough to cover her chest to the top of her thighs.

But it was what the towel was not covering which rocked him back on his heels and lighted a fire in his belly hotter than any gas boiler could manage.

Her spectacular arms and shoulders were slick and steamy from the bath and her face was flushed pink and absolutely gorgeous.

Problem was, she was winding a smaller towel around her head as she strolled out on to the landing, with her feet pushed into those silly fluffy slippers she had been wearing the night before.

This meant that her arms were lifted, stretching the towel around her chest and making it slip a little lower, then lower until it was heading for her waist.

So what if he was a boob man and proud of it?

As a gentleman, he should probably say something… but as a man? Strange how it took a few seconds before his brain took over from the other parts of his anatomy, which were waking up on their own and enjoying the view way too much.

The scent of her warm body and her sensuous movements started turning on switches which he had started to believe Alexa had turned off for good.

A hot flush of desire hit him hard and then hit him again. Apparently he still had what it took after all. That was a relief. He had started to wonder. It was hardly surprising—Antonia was absolutely stunning!

Just for a second a totally off-the-wall idea flitted through his brain.

Would she be interested in him?

A week was not long enough for anything serious but a short casual fling could be just what he needed to bring some spice back into his life. He had barely looked at another woman for the last two years but, now he was back in London, maybe it was time to find out if he was ready to share his life again.

A fling. No strings. No commitment or promises and definitely no emotional mess. Just two people enjoying one another for a casual affair.

He was certainly enjoying her right now. Thank you, Miss Baldoni!

Maybe it was time to play fair.

'Hello,' Scott said and Antonia gasped and flung herself back towards the bathroom.

'I didn't mean to startle you—' he coughed '—but...' He gestured towards the towel with his head and she immediately hoisted it higher.

'Sorry about that.' She tugged the towel a little closer to her chest. 'I don't have any hot water in my house at the moment. The plumber has the flu. Won't be back to work for another few days. And I like a bath.' Her tongue flicked out over her hot lips and every male hormone in his body pinged to attention. 'Sorry.'

'No problem.' Scott smiled and ran his hand over his

beard before saying in a casual voice, 'Stay the night if you want. You won't be disturbing me.'

'Really?' Antonia asked, her voice a high-pitched squeak.

'Sure. How about some dinner? It smells good. See you downstairs in…' Then his throat went dry as the back of the towel slipped a little, revealing a back with flawless creamy skin which was moist and warm and smelt of all of the good sweet things in his life which he'd been putting on hold since he'd divorced Alexa.

She turned slightly towards him and he noticed for the first time, in the warm ceiling lights, that Toni's eyes were not brown but a shade of copper the colour of autumn leaves. The same colour as the highlights that burnished her damp hair. And at that moment those eyes were staring very intently at him.

On another day and another time he might even have said that she was more gorgeous than merely pretty. Slender, funny and so sharp-witted that she matched him round for round.

But even the loveliest of girls had their flaws. He had learnt that from bitter experience.

Even sweet Antonia Baldoni would be hiding something from the world.

He leant closer into the light and in the harsh shadows her cheekbones were sharp angles and her chin strong and resigned. Strong. Stubborn, that was sure. But not harsh or cruel. He couldn't see that about her.

'Twenty minutes.' He grinned then waved towards her head. 'Hairdryer. Okay.'

Then he turned and almost jogged back to his room and the hot shower he wanted and the cold shower he needed.

The howling icy wind had finally eased away when Toni gave up tossing and turning from side to side and threw back the covers on the perfectly comfortable double bed in Freya's spare bedroom.

Somewhere in the house a large mechanical clock was striking every quarter hour with a musical chime but, apart from that comforting sound, the house was completely silent, as though it was a sleeping giant waiting for some magical spell to be broken.

Scott looked so exhausted and jet-lagged after dinner that he must have dropped off to sleep the minute his head hit his pillow.

The pest.

How did he expect her to sleep after walking into her coming out of the bathroom like that? She couldn't go home to have her bath—she didn't have any heating! But that didn't mean she was any less embarrassed.

To make it worse, he hadn't once mentioned seeing her half naked during one of the most awkward dinners that she had ever eaten. It was almost a relief when Scott covered a yawn with his hand and said goodnight.

She peeked out through the bedroom curtains to see that the rain had cleared, leaving a lovely clear frosty night with a bright new moon and stars. Perfect for stargazing. And, seeing that Scott was asleep…

Toni tiptoed over to the bedroom door and slowly turned the handle and peeked out through the gap. She couldn't hear any snoring or tossing but the last thing she wanted to do was wake Scott up. No repeat performances, thank you!

Slowly and quietly sneaking open the door, she stepped outside on to the landing and then crept down the staircase one stair at a time, cringing every time her slippers made the stair creak.

She could see lights from the house on the other side of the street but, apart from that, all was still calm and serene.

Toni drew back the curtains in the living room so that she could see the stars. She snuggled up on the sofa and soaked in the silence as though she were drinking the contents of a deep well of cool refreshing water. True silence like this was so rare in her life that, when it happened, she took the time to appreciate the tranquility, no matter how temporary it might be.

Especially after the roller coaster ride of the past twenty-four hours.

It was going to take a while to process everything that Scott had told her. Just when things were going so well and she'd thought this would be an easy commission and she could finally put the brushes and paints away for good.

Today had been a nightmare of such conflicting emotions. One minute she could have cheerfully taken the fee Scott was offering her...and the next?

She liked him. Heaven help her, she might even feel sorry for him.

Scott had taken on an enormous task, alone. The deal they had made could work. She knew that the longer she spent working with Scott the more she would learn about him to help her create a likeness which captured something of the real man.

But who was the real Scott Elstrom? The frostbitten lumberjack rough and tough guy who had walked into her party? Or the other Scott Elstrom who was working so tirelessly to save his heritage from the jaws of defeat and closure?

There was one thing she was certain of—everything she turned her hand to seemed to make her life more difficult instead of easier.

Even her plumber had gone down with the February flu!

The New Year had seemed so full of possibility—a white clean space just begging to be filled with activity and life and…a loud clattering sound quickly followed by a low mumble rang out from the other side of the patio doors and she practically jumped over the sofa. The sound ricocheted like a bullet around the house in the deep background silence.

Toni grabbed the sofa cushion and, holding her breath, she slowly slipped off the sofa and listened for any further signs of movement as she carefully edged her way towards the kitchen.

Perhaps she should wake up Scott?

No. Bad idea. She was embarrassed enough for one night, thank you.

There was only one thing for it—she would have to go outside and find out what was going on. And if it was a burglar, she could deal with it.

Grabbing a large wooden pepper grinder from the table with one hand, Toni carefully turned the creaking handle of the heavy doors that opened on to the patio, anxious not to make too much noise, and stepped out on to the stone patio.

The wind might have dropped but it was still freezing, with a feeling of ice in the air.

The only light was from the street lamps and local houses but, as she gingerly strolled towards the side garden in her slippers, even that background light was blocked by the house.

'Too hot? Can't blame you; it's much cooler out here.'

She practically jumped out of her skin.

There was a movement from a bench at the far end of the patio and, as her eyes became more accustomed to the low light, she saw Scott stretched out with his long legs crossed at the ankles, hands behind his head. He seemed to be fully dressed with only a light fleece jacket and she could only hope that her thin pyjamas and towelling dressing gown were not too transparent.

'Best time of the day. Here. Try this for a viewpoint. And it even has a seat.'

Scott pointed to the old wooden bench, which Toni had not even noticed on her mad dash that afternoon from the office to the kitchen. It was half hidden in a tiny arc of flowering bushes and potted plants which almost covered the surface of a small paved patio area. Completely secluded and separated from the house by a low hedge, it was a perfect private space.

'Nice spot,' Toni murmured after a few minutes to break the silence. 'Come here often?'

Scott seemed to stretch out longer and laid his head back against the wooden bench so that when he spoke it was as though his words were addressed to the sky.

'The first time I saw this garden I was fifteen years old and my parents had agreed to divorce. My mother had finally had enough of cooking meals that never got eaten because my father slept at the office and simply forgot to tell her. I can't remember a time when he ever spent more than a couple of days with us in a row. Family holidays were a joke. So out went the old Victorian museum we called home and in came this modern clean house. With heating. And lights and plumbing. It was quite a shock.'

'Tell me about it—' Toni laughed and stepped closer '—I think you just described my house.'

'Some things stayed the same.' Scott raised one arm and pointed upwards. 'The constellations didn't stomp around and cry like Freya did or collapse on the sofa exhausted every night like my poor mother. They stayed in pretty much the same place in one part of London compared to another.'

'Well—' Toni tried to keep her voice light and her heart

from exploding '—I wondered where all of those lovely diagrams came from on your maps. Scott the astronomer.'

He chuckled, his voice low, deep and resonant in the absolute stillness and silence of the night.

'Star signs were traditional on sea charts and it helps having a basic knowledge when you're out in the wild,' he replied. 'How about you? Long history of solar exploration in your family?'

'Oh, just one of my many talents,' Toni replied and was just about to make some dismissive quip when it struck her that, from the tone of his voice, he sounded different somehow. Relaxed and comfortable. At home. Unencumbered by responsibility.

So she fought back the urge to be sarcastic and strolled over towards the bench in the dark. Except her toes connected with something solid on the way.

'Ouch,' she muttered, 'what have I just banged into?'

'That would be the metal chair,' he replied with concern in his voice. 'Any damage done?'

'To my toe or your furniture?' she whispered, and then flexed her toes. 'No, I don't think so; I still have some movement. I can't speak for the other party.'

'Excellent,' he replied. 'Then please feel free to enjoy the free floor show. No charge.' Then he patted the bench next to him and Toni could have sworn that there was a certain smirk on his lips.

'Perhaps I will,' Toni said and pushed her hands into the pockets of her dressing gown as she perched on the edge of the bench and looked up into the night sky.

They both gazed skywards without speaking for a few minutes, their peace disturbed only by the sound of the traffic on the road nearby and the occasional sound of distant laughter.

She snuggled deeper into her gown. 'The sky in Alaska must be wonderful on nights like this.'

'Stunning. Have you ever seen the Northern Lights? They are the most astonishing effects. Last week I spent most of the night with the aurora as my guide.'

She shrugged and then realised that Scott probably wouldn't be able to see her. 'That makes me so jealous. I spent four days in Iceland last January and it was cloudy every single night but I still went out, just in case. My reward was a bad nosebleed and frozen eyeballs.'

Just the memory of those evenings sent a shiver down her back and she quivered and rubbed her arms.

'Feeling cold?' he asked.

'Very' she replied. 'Time for me to head back inside. Lots to do tomorrow. Oh. Make that later today.'

She heard a low grunt as Scott shuffled closer along the bench. Before she had a chance to speak, he pressed his body against the length of her side and slid his arm around her waist. A delicious glow of warmth spread across her hips and she instinctively leant sideways to enjoy the heat from his body, wrapped in his warm fleece around the front of her gown.

The whole sensation was absolutely wonderful. Solid, protective and exactly what she needed. This had been one hell of a day and she was already missing Amy so much.

'Another five minutes. We stargazers have to stick together,' Scott murmured.

He raised one arm and pointed to the bright star on the horizon below the new moon. 'On a night like this Venus and the pole star are my navigation. They get me back to base.'

'My sister is travelling in South America,' Toni replied in a low voice, thinking of Amy. 'She arrived this evening and somehow it makes me feel better to think that she is seeing the same stars as I am right now.'

'Ask me to show you a star map tomorrow.'

Toni lowered her head and watched the steam from her breath in front of her face.

'The only stars I've ever seen have been through the London haze.'

'Well, that is a shame,' Scott replied and rubbed her arms with his unbandaged hand. 'Maybe one day.'

He turned and smiled at her, and the expression on his face was so overwhelmingly full of understanding and emotion that the invisible bond that drew her to him tightened so much that it was impossible for her to resist.

Then he kissed her on the tip of her nose. And the touch of his lips was as gentle as a butterfly landing and she closed her eyes to revel in that brief moment when her skin was in contact with his.

Scott closed the tiny gap between their bodies. It seemed only natural for him to tip her chin towards him, slant his head and press his lips against hers. Softly at first, then firmer, harder, wider.

And Toni kissed him back, filling her lips and mouth with such luscious sweet warmth that any lingering resistance melted away and she moved deeper into the kiss. Eyes closed, she revelled in the sensation of falling into his mouth, their tongues touching, heads pressed together for a moment longer than she should have, before she felt Scott pull back.

His breath felt hot and fast on her neck, and Toni pressed the palms of both hands flat against the front of his fleece so that she could feel the pace of his heart beat faster to match hers as he gently lifted a strand of her hair behind one ear.

'I do have one more suggestion,' he whispered.

'Um?' Toni murmured as his fingertips slid down from her forehead to her chin in one smooth motion, as though he was unwilling to lose contact with her skin.

His fingers stilled on her chin, but she knew that his gaze was firmly locked on to her face so that when he spoke every word resonated deep into her skull. 'Why don't you stay with me tonight? I can guarantee a lot more body heat, Miss Baldoni.'

What? Her poor heart performed a crazy acrobatic dance inside her chest. The very idea was so ridiculous that it made her head spin. It was a terrible suggestion. Wasn't it? Her fingers clutched tighter to the warm, soft fleece jacket and in a moment of weakness she wondered what it would be like to skip upstairs and find out just how hot this man's body truly was.

She glared at Scott and even in the faint light she could see that he was grinning at her. As though he knew perfectly well what a temptation he was offering and was teasing her at the same time.

And he was a temptation. A serious one. She was already missing the touch of his mouth on hers and the heavy breath on her skin from the man who had the power to make her feel desirable for the first time in over a year.

Since Peter. *Peter.*

She instantly pushed Scott away with both hands flat against his chest and slid unsteadily to her feet out of the warmth of his jacket and into the cold air.

'Oh, I bet that you can. Sorry, but that is such my cue to get back to bed. My own bed. In the guest room, Mr Elstrom!'

Then, before she could change her mind, Toni stretched out and grabbed hold of the edges of his jacket and kissed him on the mouth. Hard and fast and bruising. Taking control. Calling the shots. Then she pulled away, leaving her panting for breath and maybe a lot more.

A cool breeze flitted across Toni's feet and she slipped in the flimsy mules as Scott laughed. 'Good night, Antonia.'

She half turned. 'Actually, my friends call me Toni. See you later.'

CHAPTER SEVEN

THE NARROW TERRACED house was in darkness when Toni walked up the path and turned the key in the front door. The light drizzle had turned into sleet and she was immensely grateful to step inside.

This part of Hampstead was only a few minutes away from the busy roads and the hustle and bustle of the main streets of London, but this tree-lined street seemed a world away from all of the noise and pollution.

She had waited for the bus that never came. So she had gritted her teeth and walked for thirty minutes in her smart boots, dragging her pull-along suitcase behind her rather than just stand there and wait or pay for a cab.

Waiting was for losers. Scott would never have waited—and neither would she.

She had waited for her parents to stop telling her that she was ridiculous to throw away her heritage to take up photography instead of fine art. Then waited in vain for her father to acknowledge her talent as she worked with him on his paintings, day after day, week after week until she was doing most of the work.

Slipping off her damp coat, she strolled slowly down the hallway to the kitchen, her feet dragging and her boots feeling like lead weights. Each step made the old floorboards creak and the sound echoed down the tall empty

hallway, but she had become used to each familiar sound
in this tiny house. Her faithful friends were the chiming
of the grandfather clock in the hall and the faint whistling
of the wind in the eaves.

Toni looked through the stained glass panel from the
kitchen into the artist's studio where her father used to invite sitters. In summer the house was filled with coloured
light and seemed a magical place, bright and positive and
bursting with life.

But at that moment it was dark, wet and windy and the
sleet lashed against the roof and the only light was from
the streetlight outside streaming in from the glass panel
over the front door.

And as she stood there in the kitchen, suddenly exhausted, Toni slid sideways on to a hard wooden chair at
the kitchen table with her back against the wall as though
the events of the day were too heavy to carry any longer.

What a day!

For a start, she didn't usually go around kissing men
she had just met. In fact this was a first. And the fact that
she had enjoyed it enormously didn't change the fact that
she might just have made a huge mistake.

Scott had already left for work when she got up that
morning and had been out most of the day visiting banks
and suppliers bright and early on a Monday morning. In
fact she had only seen him once when he'd let her into the
building and passed her a set of keys and he had been all
cool politeness and calm.

It was as if they had never kissed or snuggled.

So where did that leave her?

Deny it as best she could, at that moment last night
when Scott pressed his lips to hers…her poor parched
heart had soaked in every precious second of that glorious
intimacy and physical sensation like a desert in the rain.

It frightened her just how much she needed someone in her life.

But not just anyone. She wanted to be intimate with someone she could call her friend as well as her lover. Peter had never been her friend.

Scott Elstrom was the last person she wanted to fall for. He was gorgeous and she had been more than tempted to spend the night with him. But then what? A few days of fun before she went back to work?

She had never had a one-night stand in her life and this was not the best time to start.

No. It would be better if she followed Scott's example and put last night behind them and got back to being professional colleagues who would be working together for the next few days. Side by side. She could do that.

Um. *And the garden was suddenly full of a squadron of purple piglets in pink tutus singing as they flew across the sky.*

She let her head drop back and just sat there, listening to the sound of her breathing and gentle sobs in the darkness.

Pathetic!

It wasn't the dark, or the silence.

No, it was the crushing feeling of loneliness which drove her to feel sorry for herself. She had never got used to being so lonely. Amy was the only family she had left and she was currently in the depths of South America so it was silly to want to talk to her so very badly. Amy would ring or text the minute she could. She always did.

And nobody was prouder than Toni.

What had she promised Amy? This was a New Year. A fresh start.

Stupid girl! She didn't need to be alone if she didn't want to be. She had friends. Real friends who would come around in an instant if she needed them.

Toni rolled her shoulders back and was just about to pull herself to her feet when her cellphone rang out from her bag.

Amy! She scrabbled around in her bag, terrified that she would ring off before she found her phone in the near darkness, and flicked it open, instantly creating a bright panel of light. Her shoulders slumped down in disappointment. It wasn't her sister. It was an email.

With a photo of the purple underpants she had modelled last evening at her birthday party. A small smile creased her lips and Toni blinked away her tears and sniffed. Apparently Scott had found the underwear under the sofa and it had looked vaguely familiar.

Did the item belong to her or should he put it in Freya's room?

Toni giggled at the screen, tapped out a quick reply saying that she was claiming them but gift-wrapping was not necessary, thank you, and pressed the send button before she could change her mind.

That outrageous man!

But he had made her laugh and for that she was grateful.

Grinning like mad, Toni quickly scanned the other messages from her work colleagues and pals and took a sharp intake of breath. It was a perfectly friendly and chatty email from the same team she had worked with on the documentary with Peter. Apparently Peter had just joined the company's new production team, working on ideas for a five-part series on the legacy of the Raj in India. Houses and heritage. Wasn't that exciting? Why didn't she come along to the ideas meeting? Could be fun!

She almost threw the smartphone at the wall.

Peter.

Toni pressed her hand to her mouth, and then wiped away the tears from her cheeks.

Oh, what a fool she'd been.

She'd been prepared to wait for Peter to make the first move and start dating her properly. Too busy with the project at work, he had said. The film production and editing had to be perfect—but then they could relax and spend a weekend away together and tell the other people at the media company office back in London that they were a couple. Surely she could wait a few more weeks?

She had been his guilty little secret.

Sordid. Dirty. Expendable.

She had been the temporary stand-in girl he would simply throw away when he had used her enough to do his work for him. How many times had he asked her to cover up for him when he'd felt the need to sunbathe or shop?

And once their film work was over? Then he would get back to his real girlfriend, who was working on a fashion shoot and designer shows in the Caribbean.

Peter had deceived her. Tricked her. Used her for his own advantage. Amy had never liked Peter from the start and on the one occasion they had met in person had openly declared him to be a fake.

Well, that was over now. She was done with being used by other people who lied to her. That was then and this was now.

And she had waited long enough.

Lesson learnt. No more waiting. No more putting things off until later.

Toni jumped to her feet, suddenly energised and, shoving her arms into the sleeves of an old warm fleece jacket she kept by the door, she started pacing up and down to keep warm and to help clear her head.

Houses and heritage, her armpits!

What did Peter the flea know about heritage? He could

learn a few things from Scott Elstrom, and people like him, whose life was a tribute to family heritage.

Her steps slowed. Two hundred years of heritage, in fact.

A crazy idea fluttered around inside her head.

The media company she worked for was always looking for clever and special ideas and the creative director had a passion for British heritage. He had been heading up the government think tank on traditional crafts for years.

What about traditional skills such as fine British map-making?

Diving back into her bag, Toni quickly reread the email about Peter. Yes! They were using the same brilliant location scouts who had the most amazing talent for tracking down authentic buildings and sites to film historical dramas and documentaries.

They would probably faint if they walked into Elstrom Mapping!

Yes! She could see how the right director could come up with a brilliant proposal. And of course they would have to pay Scott for the exclusive use of the building for weeks, if not months!

Before she could change her mind, Toni jogged up to her freezing-cold bedroom and quickly downloaded the photographs she had taken during the past two days on to her laptop computer. It only took a few minutes to compose a few lines of explanation and her suggestion and fire off the emails and photos to the location scouts and the creative director.

The first reply came winging back before she had time to light the fire in the living room and make her hot chocolate. Every one of the scouts was pleading for more details and begging for an appointment.

Toni sat back on the sofa in front of the fire, wrapped

in a duvet, sipping her hot chocolate and then picked up her phone.

Time to call Scott. This could be fun!

Scott carefully swung Freya's hatchback around the corner from the main street and checked the name plate high on the wall of the end house. Toni had warned him that he should look out for a quiet cul de sac close to a park with trees lining the street.

The house numbers on the terraced Victorian houses were mostly hidden behind leafy evergreens or elaborate railings but as his gaze scanned the houses he spotted a bright blue and white hand-painted sign attached to a stone gate pillar. Baldoni House. This was it. He pulled into a narrow parking spot a few metres away along the street and turned off the engine and sat in the car, gathering his thoughts.

What was he doing in Hampstead at this time on a Tuesday morning? The traffic was mad, his hand was hurting and Freya's car wasn't designed for anyone over six feet tall.

He could have walked from the office in less than twenty minutes. Instead of which, it had taken him almost an hour to negotiate the road system with no help at all from Freya's new satellite navigation system. Which, for a map-maker, was not only embarrassing but incredibly frustrating.

Shrugging into his fleece jacket, Scott stepped out of the car on to the wet tarmac, which was strewn with sodden leaves, and slowly rolled back his shoulders.

The sleet and rain had cleared during the night, leaving a fresh cold morning with plenty of broken sunshine to brighten the air.

Working outdoors had made him acutely sensitive to

even the smallest change in the weather and, as he stood and gazed past the trees into the small park area, there was something in the wind that told him that this was winter's last waning steps. No more cold weather gear. No more feet of snow to plough through. No more icy winds and frozen skin.

He missed Alaska—the space and the quiet—and he missed the work. More than he'd thought possible.

Maybe this was a mistake? All it would take was one phone call and he could be on a plane back to the real life he had left behind in a couple of hours.

Inhaling sharply, Scott looked up into the branches of the trees that lined the street and focused on the sound of the birdsong instead of the incessant hum of the heavy traffic a few minutes away. A pair of grey squirrels bounced along at the foot of a large beech tree only a few metres in front of him, seeking out nuts. Playful. Spring was in the air. He had forgotten how quickly the seasons changed in Britain.

Shaking his head, Scott turned towards the narrow terraced house. It didn't look so very different from the others from the outside. Two storeys. Red brick with tall sash windows and stone window ledges. And, to his eyes, narrow. As in very narrow.

In two strides he pushed open the black wrought metal gate and crunched his way up a brick and gravel path to a covered porch. The front door was painted in the same dark blue as the window frames and a pair of bay trees in bright painted pots provided a splash of welcome green against the dark wood.

He could hear the sound of the door knocker echo inside the house as he waited on the doorstep. And waited. So this time he knocked a little harder. Still no reply.

Strange. She must have slipped out. And he had been a

bit vague when he'd said that he'd be around in the morning to collect some extra lighting equipment.

Scott was just about to head back to the car when he spotted a flash of colour out of the corner of his eye. Stepping forward, he could just see one corner of what looked like a living room from where he was standing in the porch. One step further and he had the best seat in the theatre.

The entertainment was Toni Baldoni. She was dancing. Swaying from side to side and apparently singing along to the music being fed into her ears through the wires dangling around her neck. No wonder she hadn't heard the door knocker.

Plastic crates were stacked to one side and she seemed to be moving books from the shelves as she danced.

Hands in his trouser pockets, Scott leant his back against the wall and enjoyed the moment, suddenly content to simply watch in silence as the girl he'd come to see enjoying life on her own terms. There was a fire burning in the grate and the glow from the flames lit up one side of her face in the faint morning sunlight, turning her pale skin a golden shade of flickering shadow and light on sharp cheekbones and round full lips.

How many more variations of Toni Baldoni were there?

A bright red bandana held back her hair, focusing his attention on her face. And what a face that was! The girl who had come to Elstrom Mapping was bright and intelligent and happy to challenge him on every level. Confident in her ability and fighting her corner against all of the perfectly logical reasons he could come up with why the last thing he wanted was to sit still for hours while she painted his scraggy face.

But the girl he was looking at now was completely different. It was as if a weight had been taken from her shoulders and she was free to be herself in her own space. Her fine cheekbones glowed and a big smile creased her face, which positively beamed with warmth and happiness.

Yes. That was the difference. She looked happy. Joyous, even. High on life.

With a dress sense to match her mood.

Toni was wearing what looked to him like a flying suit, only the strangest one he had ever seen. It looked as though some toddler had melted every crayon in the box and sprayed the whole lot over a pair of workman's overalls. It was astonishing. Put that with a brunette who was dancing across the floor and the whole picture was worth taking the time to admire.

In fact he could do better than that. He could try and capture some of that happiness.

Tugging his smartphone out of his jacket pocket, Scott lifted it to his eye but the second he pressed the camera button he knew that he had made a mistake.

The flash went off. Toni immediately whirled around and came to the window to find out what was going on. And saw him. Ogling her.

The expression on her face would have broken the camera lens. *Oops.*

Then he made it worse by giving a casual wave.

Toni stood with her hands wrapped around a copy of an old encyclopaedia for several seconds, staring at Scott in disbelief, before she whirled around, tossed the book on to the sofa and lifted the ear pieces out and turned off her music system.

Her heart was thumping so hard that she was certain that it would beat out of her chest and that Scott would be able to hear it on the porch.

Oh, no. She hadn't expected him to show up this early.

She wasn't dressed for visitors and especially not him! She had planned to get showered and blow-dried and nicely dressed before he turned up to collect the lighting equipment.

Plan B.

A low groan of exasperation escaped her lips and, with a quick shake of her head, she padded out to the hallway in her stocking feet.

Catching a glance at her reflection in the hall mirror wasn't a good idea but there wasn't much she could do about that now, and he had already seen her, so…chin up, smile on. She could carry this off…couldn't she?

With her head high, Toni flung open her front door, ready to give Scott a lesson on manners.

The words caught in her throat as she gulped in a breath of air in startled shock.

She had been too busy reacting to seeing him standing there to pay attention to what he really looked like, but as the morning sunlight hit the porch she was hit by the full-on splendour that was the cleaned up version of Scott Elstrom.

He was wearing a smart cashmere jacket and dark trousers, a pale blue button-down collar shirt which only made his deep tan more pronounced and he had done something to his hair. *Washed it.*

Her stomach turned over just to look at him and her heart was doing things which were probably dangerous to her blood pressure.

She had thought that Scott was attractive when he'd first walked in on her birthday party, and he had changed his shirt yesterday at the office, but this version leaning against her porch was from another planet.

A planet of hunky handsomeness where the adult males

were all tall, blond and had neatly trimmed beards which only highlighted their square jaws and long straight noses.

His cheekbones were so taut they might have been sculpted. But it was his mouth that knocked the air out of her lungs and had her clinging on to the door frame for support. A plump lower lip smiled wide above his cleft chin, so that the bow was sharp between the smile lines. It was a mouth made for smiling.

The corners of those amazing blue eyes crinkled slightly in his deeply tanned skin and Toni realised that he had been watching her. The warmth of that smile seemed to heat the air between them. It was so full of genuine charm and delight that she knew, no matter what, this was the smile that would stay with her for a long time.

This smile was for her. And her heart leapt. More than a little. But just enough to recognize that the blush of heat racing through her neck and face were not only due to the flames that had been warming her back.

That killer smile and those blue eyes came together in one single look that could charm anything in its path and knock it senseless. There was no escape. She was hit with the full blast.

The top two buttons of his pale blue shirt gaped open as the fabric stretched over a broad chest and revealed a hint of deeply tanned skin, and more than a few dark chest hairs.

He was stunning.

Oh, no. Do not stare at his chest. Just don't.

The pounding in her chest was simply because she had been taken by surprise—that was all. Trying desperately to regain some kind of control over feelings that were so new and raw, Toni stepped forward to meet him.

Luckily he spoke first, his voice low and husky in the quiet garden as he smiled and reached out his hand. Toni felt his long cold fingers clasp around hers for only a few seconds before she released him. The calloused surfaces of his fingers rasped against her skin on the back of her hands. Gentle but firm.

'Good morning. Apologies if I startled you but I tried the front door and there was no answer.' He made a point of checking his gold wristwatch. 'And I am early. I hope that isn't a problem.'

Oh, no. No problem at all. It was perfectly normal for her to welcome clients who looked like Viking gods when she was wearing her grungiest painting overalls!

She should be annoyed. But look at the man!

Toni inhaled deeply, straightened her back and managed to find her voice at last as she smiled back at him. 'No problem at all. Please do come in out of the cold. I have a fire going in the living room and hot coffee on the table. Want to join me? Because I can't wait to hear what you think about my idea. You're going to be in the movies! Isn't that exciting?'

'You're serious, aren't you?' Scott said as he followed Toni into the house. 'You really think that TV companies will want to keep Elstrom locked in some strange hibernation so that they can use it as a film set?'

'Absolutely,' she replied. 'There are plenty of location scouts who would love to use the building as a movie set for documentaries or dramas set in wartime or 1930s Britain.' Then she winced and bared her teeth. 'No offence but it is a bit of a time warp when you walk in those doors. And you don't even have to clear the rooms because they will do all that for you. Scott? Are you listening?'

Listening? He was far too busy trying to cope with the sensory overload that was the Baldoni house. The entire living room was more like an expressionist art gallery than a family home.

Colour was piled on tones and shades of colour. The walls were covered in heavy red wallpaper with a faint gold pattern embossed in what looked to him like random patterns. Not that he could see too much of the wallpaper. There must have been at least twenty pictures on the walls, of all shapes and sizes. Portraits of people in various styles of dress, landscapes, fruit and flowers. It was all there on the walls of this tiny room, about the size of Freya's kitchen.

And then there were the fabrics. Curtains, sofa and cushions. All red, all different, all bursting with pattern and shades of crimson and gold trim.

Scott couldn't imagine a greater contrast between the cold grey February street outside and the shock of this space. It was like a rich tent in the desert. Exotic and luxuriant and bursting with interest and textures.

'Wow—' he coughed '—this is remarkable. Sorry, but my poor scientific brain is struggling to cope. I know that you come from a family of artists but I had no idea that you had to surround yourself with so many colours.'

Toni laughed and shrugged. 'My grandparents bought the place when Hampstead was famous for the artist colonies. The Baldoni family were very popular and they bought paintings from their friends and even a few clients. You know that store room at the back of the Elstrom mapping room? I have one of those upstairs to cope with the overflow.'

'There's more?'

'Oh, this is nothing. You should have seen the place before Amy and I started to declutter over the Christmas holiday. Black coffee okay?'

'Please,' Scott replied and strolled around the room,

picking up hand-painted china ornaments then peering at the stack of books that Toni had been looking at when he'd spied on her through the window.

'Doing some spring-cleaning?' he asked, glancing at her over one shoulder. Her answer was the kind of laugh that made the glass in the windows rattle.

'Cleaning? Oh, if only that was all I had to do.' Then she must have spotted the confused look on his face and she passed him a coffee with a grin.

'Amy and I have decided to rent the place out while she is away at university. I plan to do more travelling for work and she won't be here and we need the loot. One of my neighbours gave me all of the details and a couple of agencies have been around. Strange how they all say the same thing. It seems that there are a few small things I need to do before I can rent this house to anyone.'

Toni squeezed her thumb and forefinger together. 'Very small. Nothing really. Ha!'

She collapsed down on the sofa, which was covered with a dust sheet, and picked up her coffee mug and waved it towards the bookcases.

'Fix the plumbing. Put in a new bathroom. And the big one? Get rid of ninety per cent of the books and paint-ings and the rest of the clutter and paint the walls a beige, creamy buttermilk-type colour. Neutral. Bland. Plain. In fact the colour of the walls in Freya's kitchen. It looks great in a modern house. Here? Not so sure.'

'No alternative? Rent it to art lovers? No? Ah, then I can see the problem. There does seem to be a lot of—what did you call it?—clutter?'

'You have no idea. Elstrom was easy compared to this. Let's just say that your father wasn't the only one who didn't want to change things in a hurry.'

She sniffed and looked from side to side. 'When you've

used this room every day it comes as a bit of a shock when other people see it differently. But they're right. I need to clear the room, get rid of the paintings and wallpaper and start all over again…' Her voice faded away. 'So that is what I plan to do. A new start in a nice new bright home. All white and fresh. Oh, yes.'

'What are you going to do with it all? Some of these paintings must be valuable.'

'That's why I have a professional lighting rig. Every piece has to be photographed for the insurance and then put into storage or sold.' Toni exhaled sharply. 'Then it's going to take weeks to redecorate and work out what to do with boxes of ancient books.' She glanced up at Scott. 'Sorry. Too much to do. Not enough time. Sound familiar?'

'Very.' He grinned and hooked his arm over the back of the sofa and looked from side to side. 'Are all the rooms like this?'

'Oh, no. This is tidy. The only reason I'm working in here is the fire.' She laughed. 'No plumbing. No heating. Electric heaters are great but an open fire is bliss.'

Scott put down his mug with a clatter. 'I thought that you meant the hot water wasn't working! You should have told me! Freya's house is so hot I can hardly breathe and she hates it when I turn the thermostat down. Please. Come back and stay there until you have heating.'

Toni smiled at him. 'Now you're being kind. But this is my space and, as you can see, I have a fire and lots to do.' Then she took a breath and sat back on the sofa and brought her knees up to her chest. 'There is one thing I find curious. You keep saying Freya's house. Isn't that your home too?'

The reply stuck in Scott's throat. *It was until I got married and moved into my own place. Alexa got the apart-*

ment in the divorce. I certainly didn't want it. Not after she admitted taking Travis there.

Toni must have seen the expression on his face and immediately held up one hand. 'Forget it. I am far too nosey and you are here for the lighting rig. It's all ready for us in the studio and…'

Scott rested one hand lightly on Toni's knee and looked into her face.

'When our mother moved to Paris I shared the house with Freya until I bought my own place with my fiancée. Two years ago I moved to Alaska and my former wife got the apartment as the divorce settlement. Since then Freya has kept my old bedroom in case I needed it. But home? No. It's not my home. Not any longer.'

'I am so sorry. About the divorce and about the apartment. That's hard to imagine. Amy and I have already organized a tiny studio flat we're going to call home in a few months. We need that.'

'Everyone's different. I'm on the move so much I don't need a permanent base. The only place that I have ever really called home was the massive Victorian mansion in north London that I grew up in.' He smiled across at Toni. 'It wasn't that much different from this house. Bigger rooms meant more space to clutter up. And my dad was certainly up to the challenge. Believe me, this place would fit him like a glove.'

Scott froze and took a few seconds to take in everything, from the Victorian glass lamp shades to the leather-bound books and heavy gold-framed landscapes.

'He would love it here,' Scott whispered and his two middle fingers tapped out a beat on the hard cover of a book about Victorian watercolours.

Then they stopped and he lifted his chin and stared at

Toni, who had started lifting smaller books down from the bookcase on the other side of the fireplace.

'It's a shame that we don't have an elevator at the office. My dad can't move back to his top floor studio until he has more control of his legs.'

Toni glanced at him over one shoulder. 'Oh, that is a shame. Will he move in with Freya?'

'No. He hates modern houses. That's one of the reasons why he stays in Italy. I do have an idea for somewhere he could rent...but it would all depend on you.'

Toni put down her book and turned around and sat on the edge of the sofa. 'Me? Why? Do you need a second opinion?'

Scott slid forward and rested both hands on his knees so that his whole body pointed towards her.

'Not exactly. You see, I think this little house would be perfect for my dad, and for me. I can't stay at Freya's, I know that now. Which means that I need somewhere to rent for the next six months...and he needs somewhere quiet but close to his friends in London. And old school. Yes, I think this could be the perfect place for us.'

Scott grinned up at Toni, who was staring at him with her mouth half open. 'What do you say, Toni? Will you rent your house to the Elstrom boys?'

Toni stared into his face for a second in total silence, with an expression that was part shock and horror and part bewilderment.

'You want to rent my house?'

He nodded once and gestured towards her with one hand. 'I can offer you top rates and a good deposit if that's what you're worried about and I promise that we won't trash the place.'

Toni's jaw had dropped slightly, which probably meant

that she was at least not dismissing the idea out of hand, so Scott dived in quickly to seal the deal. 'Think of me as your ideal tenant. Hardly here. Does the washing-up when he has to and is fairly orderly. And my dad has this thing for old books and paintings. He may not be the best businessman in the world but I know that he could feel at home here.'

'Scott, you are not making any sense whatsoever. You have only been here five minutes! How do you know what the rest of the house is like? The studio is stacked to the ceiling with canvases and painting stuff and the bathroom is going to be all modern and white and flash when it's done. Your dad might hate it.'

'Good. I like the sound of that already. As for the rest of the house? I would love a tour.'

And for the first time that morning Scott lifted his chin towards the window so that she could see his face in the sunlight instead of shadow.

Although his mouth was turned into a gentle half smile there was a deep crease between his eyebrows and, as she looked closer, the deep shadows under his eyes told her that he had probably had less sleep than she had. Those stunning, hypnotic blue eyes scanned her face over and over again, as though he was looking for a sign of how she was feeling about him.

And they looked at each other in silence for what seemed like minutes.

Then both of them started talking at the same time.

'Ladies first,' Scott chuckled, breaking the crackling electric current that was in the air between them.

'Okay,' Toni replied. 'Talk to me. What's this really all about, Scott?'

Scott looked at her then leant closer. 'My father needs something positive in his life. He's come out of this second divorce with health problems and the business has collapsed around him. We are totally different people in every way. But right now? I wouldn't mind spending some time with him when he comes back to London.'

He looked around and flashed her a grin. 'Sharing a house like this would be a blast. It reminds me of the early family house we used to have when we felt more like a family than strangers that passed in the hallway from time to time. I mean it. He would love it here. And think of it this way.' He flicked one hand into the air. 'Less clutter to sort out. He likes the clutter.' Then his overly confident smile faded a little. 'We haven't been very good friends since I left the business. Things were totally crazy back then and things were said which cannot be unsaid. Maybe it's time to move on.'

'By sharing this tiny house? I don't know, Scott.'

He flicked a tongue over his lips. 'If this is about the other night, I owe you an apology. I should not have kissed you and I am sorry that it has put us into an awkward situation.'

Toni took a deep breath and looked into his face. His last few words had come gushing out in one long rush and she knew how hard they must have been to say. 'No—it's nothing to do with that. You don't owe me an apology,' she replied. 'I was right there and I may even have kissed you at one time. Let's call it evens.'

Scott shook his head. 'I think I do. We had both worked hard, it was a lovely evening and I got caught up in the moment.'

He lifted both hands from the table. 'It certainly wasn't planned, but I don't want there to be any confusion. You are one hell of a beautiful woman and I cannot guarantee that I'll be able to keep my hands off you.'

Scott looked up at her and this time his face was pale

and serious and each and every one of the frown lines were frozen into sharp relief.

'I can understand it if you want to hit me over the head with one of those heavy books, but I'm hoping that you can forgive me and my overactive libido enough to work with me as a colleague over the next few days and think about renting me your home. How about it, Toni? Willing to give me a chance?'

Toni stared at Scott long enough to see beads of perspiration on his forehead.

It was probably only minutes but in the silence of the room all she had to listen to was the background soundtrack of birdsong and the thumping of her heart.

Because Scott had just told her in his own way that he felt just as much for her as she was feeling for him. He was trying to create some distance between them to protect them both from the pain of some crazy love affair.

And he clearly had no idea that she could see it in his face. And, if anything, his words only served to bind them more closely together instead of driving them apart. He was doing this for her as much as himself.

Toni pushed up from the sofa and put her coffee mug on the table, aware that Scott was still watching her every move.

'You'd better see the studio first. It would make a perfect workroom for your dad.'

CHAPTER EIGHT

'I KNOW. It's fantastic news, Freya! My friend must have taken fifty photos yesterday before she made up her mind but I had a feeling that she would, fast! What was that? How did Scott react to the news?'

Toni grinned and scanned through some of the images on her camera one-handed. 'Your brother gave that poor woman the benefit of his full-on charm offensive. I have never seen him so cooperative. He even shaved a little and changed into a smart shirt! I know! Amazing. She was putty in his hands. But it worked. We have a deal! I am so pleased for you both. In fact, Scott was so relieved that the building is safe for the rest of the year that he took off into the snow to bring back coffee and doughnuts. It's a dangerous mission but he refused to be deterred.'

Freya's laughter echoed down the phone as she described how it was positively balmy in Rome but she would be back in a few weeks to do more to help out. With a quick promise to meet up as soon as they could, Toni closed the call and put down the handset. Her fingers lingered on the phone as she breathed out slowly.

In a week and a half she would be back at work in some freezing photographic studio and this world of old maps and charts and wood-panelled walls would be a distant memory.

But what about Scott?

He was serious about renting out her house so there was no hope that she could be free of him. And that was the problem. She didn't want to be free of the man.

They had worked side by side over the past four days and the more time she spent with Scott the more she liked him.

Scott Elstrom was clever, quick and actually willing to listen to her ideas, which made a nice change from her normal work where she was still the minion girl Friday who did most of the running about for the guys with the professional qualifications and experience. Scott treated her like an equal.

The hard, brash exterior was a total front—the armour he wore to get by in his world. Gut instinct told her that he had been badly hurt at some time but she wasn't going to pry. If he wanted to tell her about it he would if and when he was ready. She still wasn't sure what his true reasons for coming back to Elstrom Mapping were but he was certainly working hard to save the business.

In four days, and with fingers which were still strapped up and obviously hurting, Scott had helped her to clear the main office, made an inventory of everything that had been left behind in the mapping room where the few staff used to work, and had passed her the first box of items to photograph.

Yesterday's visit from the location scout had been the icing on the cake!

She'd loved this old building and had immediately seen the potential for several historical documentaries and dramas already commissioned during the year.

It was a start and meant Scott could get to work on the inventory without having to worry about the lights being turned off. He might even be able to afford to replace the central heating boiler and the flaky electrics which made the lights flicker on and off.

Lifting her camera to her eyes, Toni captured a few images of this amazing room with all the rows of tools and the huge drawing tables.

She heard his footsteps pound up the staircase before the front door closed and slowly turned towards the office as Scott came bounding in and dropped his bakery bag on to the table in front of his office window.

There were snowflakes caught in his hair and on the shoulders of his coat and as Toni stepped into the office he lifted his chin and looked out of the window with a wistful smile on his face. As though he was looking out at the light snow and thinking of other people and other places.

Her breath caught in her throat and she pressed the shutter and kept on pressing it. Over and over again.

The tingles ran down her arms to her fingers. That was it. That was the image she had been looking for.

There was always a moment when she knew that she had taken the perfect shot of her subject. Sometimes it took days of careful staging to make the subject feel comfortable in the setting and other times it was completely spontaneous. Sometimes it never happened and they had to make the best of what they had taken.

Not today. The picture she was going to paint was already forming in her mind and she could practically see the way her paint was going to capture his swept back blond hair and dark eyebrows, damp now with melting snow.

Sniffing back a wave of emotion, Toni lowered her camera and smiled as Scott turned to face her.

It was as if every cell in her body was suddenly totally fascinated by the freckles across the bridge of his long straight nose and the way the crease lines at the sides of his eyes were white against his tanned skin.

Scott Elstrom was not a handsome man at all. He was gobsmacking gorgeous.

His presence jumped out at her, grabbed her by the bra straps and pulled her with such force that she could almost feel her body leaning forward towards him.

'Hey—' he grinned '—ready for coffee?'

A shot of pure lust hit her hot and wet in all of the wrong places.

Oh, my. Not now. Please, not now. This is not good.

'You bet,' she whispered in a quivering voice. 'Any time.'

He shot her a worried look. 'Sore throat? You have to watch these colds this time of year.'

Oh, please don't be nice to me, she willed. *Focus on the work instead.*

'Not at all,' Toni replied, lifting her chin. 'Just chattering too long on the phone to Freya. She's so pleased with the location deal she just couldn't wait to call.'

'Damn right,' Scott said and shrugged off his jacket. 'You did a great job, so today we have chocolate cream éclairs instead of doughnuts. Prepare for the sugar rush!'

His shirtsleeves were still rolled up and Toni couldn't stop herself from focusing on how the blond hairs on his arms prickled to attention as he dived into the bag and pulled out the coffees and pastries.

'Don't you mean that we did a great job? I only made that first call. It was your idea to dig out all of those old photos of the building and I know she loved those sepia prints with the horse-drawn carriages outside. Light bulbs were flashing inside her head with every new image.'

Toni reached out and wrapped a napkin around the piece of iced pastry which was in great danger of ooz-

ing fresh cream all over his desk and tried to ignore the
way that Scott's lips closed around the top of his coffee.
'The shameless charm offensive didn't hurt either, you
old smoothie.'

Scott replied with a low grunt but she could tell from
the slight flush at the back of his neck that he was slightly
embarrassed. 'So what have you been up to?' he asked,
rapidly changing the subject between slurps of coffee and
bites of pastry.

'Box number four. The instruments have been photographed from every angle and I was just about to start
work on that stunning map you prepped this morning.
Want to take a look?'

He nodded and, picking up his coffee, strolled out of
the office and followed her into the map room, brushing
sugar from his fingers as he walked.

'So tell me about this sea chart,' Toni said as she ad-
justed her camera settings on the tripod. 'The colours are
amazing. Is it all hand-painted?'

Scott looked up from his coffee. 'Absolutely. I'm working on the catalogue entry next.' He pointed towards the
mapping table where he had unfurled the leather scroll
for Toni to photograph. 'This is a portolan from a Spanish
cartographer who had a workshop on the Canary Islands
in about 1730. He made it his business to collect every
scrap of information from the captains and navigators who
stopped there on the way back from trading journeys to
the Caribbean or Far East. Each map took months but they
were traded for huge sums.'

'I can understand why,' Toni replied, looking down
her viewfinder. 'Such beautiful workmanship and what
tiny writing. I will need to do something special for those
sections.'

She stepped back and planted a hand on each hip as she

tilted her head. 'Are you going to sell it?' she asked as she walked around the chart and studied it from every angle.

Scott got slowly to his feet and stood next to her, the sleeve of his shirt bristling against her top as he pointed to dark marks on the corners of the leather and a strange stain right in the middle of the chart. 'If the price is right. My father intended to restore these pieces before he put them on the market. There is a specialist map dealer who begged us to sell it about ten years ago. A Russian oligarch wanted an original sea chart for his new office in London but my dad refused. It was too precious to him.'

A deep sigh made Toni look up at Scott and he smiled back at her.

'I love my father, Toni, but he is clueless when it comes to people. His world centres on books and research studies. He has published brilliant works on the history of sea charts. They're amazing! Elstrom men were sea captains whose mission was to create navigational charts on a sea journey and detailed land maps when they arrived on the east coast of America or Canada or around the top of the world into Russia. That was how the company got started. Men and paper and a hard life in the worst conditions where a lot of the crew didn't make it back. So my father used the family histories and documents to create a personal history of the exploration and how map-making is part of who we are.'

'What will your father do when he's feeling better?' Toni asked.

'What he loves to do. Restore charts and maps. Research books and be the expert he was always intended to be. He was never cut out to be a businessman and certainly not a husband or father. He is clueless when it comes to family life.'

'What do you mean, clueless? Freya seems to get on okay with him.'

'Two marriages and two divorces. No happy ending for anyone.'

Scott rolled his shoulders back as though he was trying to stretch out the knots from sitting hunched over his laptop for several hours. 'The only reason this collection is still in the archive at all was that my predecessor had no clue what was inside the leather scroll tubes and my father was too busy to explain. The really valuable pieces were sold about a year ago to pay the staff. They were top quality pieces in perfect condition. No catalogue needed.'

'Your predecessor?' Toni wrapped her hand on the tripod and turned to look at Scott. 'Did your dad employ a business manager? You haven't mentioned that before.'

There was a sharp cough and a low grunt from across the table. 'Not exactly. My stepbrother joined the company two years ago straight out of business school. Travis ran the business when I was working overseas. He was a disaster as a man and as a manager.'

Toni nodded very slowly. 'Ah. Stepbrother. That must have been difficult, for you and your dad.' Then she sniffed and waved her hand from side to side. 'I get it. You're back to show this Travis who is the better man. A lot of pressure on you to get the job done, but that makes perfect sense now.'

Instantly the air temperature seemed to drop several degrees and she pressed her lips together and pretended to be extra fascinated in the sea chart.

'Are you always so intuitive?' Scott asked in a low, hoarse voice but there was just enough humour in it that she felt that she could breathe again.

'Always. Only one of my many special gifts. Think of

it as a free bonus with the portrait painter and photographer special package deal.'

He gestured with his head towards the camera as though signalling that he wanted to change the subject. 'Speaking of which. How are we doing?'

Toni smiled and walked around to the laptop computer and full-sized monitor that she had brought from home. 'Why don't you take a look? I think this catalogue design works, but you're the expert!'

She perched on the end of the high stool and opened up the online digital catalogue that they had agreed was the best format for displaying the inventory. The images could easily be enlarged so that all of the stunning detail popped out in full colour alongside a full description and history for each piece.

Toni felt Scott's arm press against hers as he bent down to look at the screen so that as she turned to speak their faces were only inches apart.

His tanned forehead might be furrowed, rough and creased with life but his mouth was soft and wide.

Lush.

He already had the slightest hint of stubble at eleven a.m., so the rest of his body must be... No, she couldn't think about what was below the glimpse of blond chest hairs curling out from the V of his shirt.

He half opened his mouth to say something, grinned and then changed his mind.

Her brain screamed out that this was a huge mistake and that she should tell him the presentation needed a lot more work and that she needed to get back to the photography. But her heart was too busy getting worked up over the boyish smile on his face and the very manly look in those eyes that were smiling at her.

He was dazzling!

As she perched on the stool, his head was only inches from her face, her bosom pressed against his shirt. In a fraction of a second, Toni was conscious that his hand had slid slowly around her waist, moving under her top so his fingertips could feel the heat of her warm skin. She felt something connect in her gut, took a deep breath and watched words form in that amazing mouth.

'Did you know that Freya has a passion for baking?'

'She never mentioned it,' Toni whispered as Scott stepped a little closer into the gap between her legs.

Suddenly she wasn't so sure that her decision to wear a skirt and leggings today instead of her usual black trousers was such a good idea.

Because, as Scott moved closer, her skirt started to hitch higher up her legs and her hands were too busy holding her up to do anything about it.

'Cakes, mainly. Do you like cake, Toni?'

'Oh, yes. I love cake, especially...chocolate,' Toni replied, but the words were driven from her mind as Scott's fingers wound up into her hair and then the base of her skull. His gaze followed the line of his hand as though her hair was the most fascinating thing that he had ever seen.

His fingers slid forward and stroked her cheek with the gentlest of touches.

'You have cream and éclair on your face,' Scott whispered and, leaning forward, he raised one finger and brushed it along her upper lip. Then, as she watched, riveted, he slowly ran the tip of his tongue across his chocolate-covered fingertip.

It only took a fraction of a second but it was the hottest thing Toni had ever seen in her life. So hot she couldn't help herself taking a sharp breath in some feeble attempt to cool her suddenly burning cheeks.

'Perhaps we should stick to the doughnuts in future?' she squeaked. 'Messy eater.'

'I'll risk it.' He grinned and followed the outline of her jaw with his thumb.

Scott slanted his head and slid closer and just for one second she thought that he was going to kiss her neck.

Instead, she felt a breath of warm sweet air from his soft lips against her cheek.

And every hair on her body instantly stood to attention.

Before she could change her mind, Toni rested both hands lightly on his hips so that the scent and sensation of his body could warm every cell in hers before she finally pulled her head back.

She knew without looking that her nipples were alive and proud and probably doing crazy things to the front of her top, but she truly did not care.

Scott looked straight at her, his chest responding to his faster breathing, and whispered, 'Chocolate works for me,' before sliding his hands down the whole length of her back, the pressure drawing her forward as he moved his head into her neck and throat, kissing her with just the barest contact of his lips on her collarbone, then up behind her ears, his hands moving up and down in a gentle caress of both sides of her back, inside her sweater. As though he wanted to find out what her skin tasted like without the chocolate and cream chaser.

The stubble on his chin and sideburns made her burn with instant fire, and instinct rather than sensible thought took over.

And chocolate was not what Toni was thinking about. At all.

For a moment their eyes locked together.

The need in his took her breath away and left her floundering, helpless.

What if he wanted her as much as she wanted him at this minute?

That could only spell trouble. For both of them.

Toni tried to break the mood by looking away first.

And then she made the fatal mistake of glancing back and fell dizzyingly into Scott's startling blue flecked eyes. Eyes which called to her with a message that her heart could not ignore.

I like you. A lot.

Doomed.

Without a second's hesitation, she leaned forward just an inch and started to angle her head so that their noses wouldn't clash, their eyes still locked. His tongue moistened his upper lip, and she instinctively did the same. His eyes glanced from her mouth back to her eyes as his hand came up to cradle the back of her head, smoothing down the hair, caressing the warm skin between her neck and ear. And suddenly she wanted—needed—to crush her mouth against his and taste his sweetness and life and passion.

She could sense that her breathing sped up in anticipation for his kiss, her eyes half closed at the pleasure to come. *She wanted him to kiss her.*

But what he did instead made kissing seem tame in comparison.

Scott's fingers moved down from her waist on to the rough tweed fabric of her trendy skirt until they reached her exposed leggings-covered thighs.

Toni breathed out a sigh of shuddering delight as his palms cupped her thighs, his thumbs caressing back and forth on the sensitive area on the inside of her legs, moving just a little higher with each caress.

She blinked up into Scott's face and he smiled at her

with an expression that told her everything that she needed to know.

This man knew exactly what he was doing and how her body was reacting to his touch. But she wasn't the only one. His breathing was matching hers, hot and fast and snatched between gasps.

Just to prove the point, his gaze locked on to hers and his hands pushed her skirt just high enough for him to step closer so she could feel just how much his body was enjoying the moment.

Somewhere inside her head a voice was telling her that she should tell him to stop. Soon. Very...*oh, Lord*...soon. But maybe not straight away. Because this felt way too good to stop.

Toni was just about to arch her back over the drawing table when Scott suddenly moved his hands out from under her skirt, pressed them on to the table, stepped back and whispered, 'I have an idea.'

An idea? What? Now?

Licking her lips and forcing her brain to form something close to sense took a second but eventually Toni managed to whisper, 'Great. Although I was hoping that you might have more than just the one.'

'Ah, but this is a classic. How would you like to be my date for dinner this evening?'

What?

Toni felt as though someone had just thrown a bucket of cold water over her and she instantly pushed her bottom off the stool and tugged her skirt down.

'A date? You? Me? Are you serious?'

'Is that so outrageous?'

'No. I mean yes,' Toni blustered, desperately trying to come up with an excuse why she could not, dare not put her heart on the line again. 'Technically, I'm working for you. An employee, in fact. And you have a girlfriend. You told me about the girl you left behind in Alaska the other day in the coffee shop. I'm sure that your lovely blue-eyed Dallas wouldn't be too happy with that idea. I don't date other girl's boyfriends. Ever.'

Scott paused for a moment, grinned then pulled out his wallet and handed her a photograph. 'Good to know. Toni, meet Dallas.'

'Oh, you have to be kidding me? You keep a photo of…a very handsome husky dog.' Toni peered at it, rolled her eyes and passed the snapshot of the dogsled back to its owner. 'Tease. Dallas is one of your sled dogs, isn't she?'

'Hell, no.' Scott grinned. 'Dallas is my lead girl. She runs the rig. If she doesn't want to tug and run?' He sliced the air with his hand. 'We're grounded.' Then a warm loving smile crept up out of nowhere and hit her with its full power. 'But when she moves? That girl is poetry in motion. And smart. We get on just fine.'

'So I see.' Toni smiled. 'Well, it's obvious that any girl would have to work hard to compete with the lovely Dallas. That's a special relationship.' She sucked in air between her teeth. 'I wouldn't want to come between a man and his dog.'

Scott scowled at her then pressed his lips together, winced, and then slapped the heel of his hand to his forehead as he took several steps back towards the door. 'You already have a boyfriend. Of course you do. How stupid of me.'

He gave her a short bow. 'Apologies. I jumped to conclusions. Another one of those flaws I was talking about. I only hope your boyfriend doesn't turn up at the house and thump me for asking his girl out.'

There was just enough of a change in his voice to make her look up. Unless he was a very good actor and she was completely misreading the signals, she saw a glimmer of genuine regret and disappointment cross that handsome face before he covered it up.

Interesting.

Decision time. Pretend she was seeing someone and lie through her teeth...or not.

'You're safe. I broke up with someone a year ago and right now I'm on my own. What I meant was that I'm between boyfriends and I don't feel comfortable with starting a serious relationship right now. But thanks again for the invitation.'

It was astonishing to see how fast Scott could switch on that killer smile.

'Ha. So you are single. That makes two of us.' He looked at her quizzically, eyebrows high. 'But who said anything about a serious relationship? What I'm talking about is a fling. A sweet, short and fun fling.'

'A fling? Why on earth would you want a fling with me? You could have your pick of girls to fool around with.'

He stepped closer and ran his hands up both sleeves of her jacket and smiled as his gaze locked on to her eyes. 'I've been through one very difficult divorce and since then my focus has been totally on my work. The last thing I want is to rush into that sort of commitment again. But I would like to get to know you better. A lot better. Maybe even get used to the idea that I can start looking for love again. Do you understand that?'

'Looking for love again? Yes. Yes, of course I understand that. Isn't that what we all want?'

Scott gave a small shoulder shrug. 'Maybe. But in the meantime we're both adults who understand the difference between a casual arrangement and a long-term relationship. This way, we can have the benefits. Without the messy complications.'

Then the tone of his voice cooled. 'But I'll be back in Alaska by the autumn. I can't promise you anything but a good time for the next few months and I need to know that you understand that very clearly. No confusion or re-criminations. A fling. Short and sweet. Now. What can I do to tempt you to take up my offer?'

'Oh, Scott,' she replied, shaking her head. 'You're temptation on legs.'

A smile that could defrost icebergs warmed the air. 'It's been said. And you're a lovely girl, Toni. We seem to make a great team at work. Now that has to say something.'

Make a great team at work! Oh, Scott, if you only knew. That was the worst thing that you could possibly have said.

Those were the precise words that Peter had used, right before he'd whisked her off to his hotel room and off her feet. She had fallen hard and fast in weeks not months. Blind to all the warning signs that screamed out to her not to go there. Her head full of dreams of a wonderful future working together. And all the time he was using her to get the work done and be his dirty little fling at the same time.

Six months with Scott Elstrom? Oh, no.

Toni chuckled under her breath and slowly slid out of the warmth of his embrace, even though it killed her to do it.

'Lovely and convenient! Sheesh. I'm the one who actually pushed to work in your office and take your photograph.'

She flipped her right hand over from side to side. 'Painter. Client.' Then she blew out hard and shook her head. 'So many great artists have fallen into that trap. Disaster waiting to happen.'

Then she gave a casual shoulder shrug. 'Sorry, Scott.

My answer is thank you but no. You're going to have to work harder and find yourself another fling partner.'

She braced her back and shoulders and lifted her chin as Scott formed a reply, but was saved by her cellphone.

It was Amy's personal ringtone.

Great timing, sis!

'Sorry,' she whispered to Scott, who was glaring at the phone as though he wanted to toss it out of the nearest window. 'Amy…Peru. I should really answer it. Really sorry.'

It took a moment for her to slide her body sideways and out of the circle of his arms but even as she lifted the phone she could feel his gaze burning a hole in her back.

Tugging down the hem of her top as if Amy could see her, she opened the call and, before she could say a word, an entire orchestral chorus of *Happy Birthday* belted out at huge decibels into the quiet room.

Oh, great! Amy had sent her a musical birthday card to add to the surprise birthday present of a tiny locket that she had left for their neighbour to deliver that morning.

Scrabbling with her phone, she quickly turned it off, took a breath and turned sideways to look at Scott, who was standing with his arms folded and a lazy grin plastered all over his face.

'Today is your birthday? You might have mentioned that earlier. I could have brought back extra chocolate.'

'I had my party on Saturday, remember? At Freya's house. No big deal.'

'Oh, no—' he shook his head and pushed out his lips '—you don't get away that easy. I would fail in my duty if I didn't take you out for a birthday dinner. What time do you want me to pick you up for your date?'

My date?

Her heart was thumping so loudly he could probably hear it from where he was standing. He smelt wonderful, his touch sent her brain spinning and he was so handsome that her heart melted just looking at him.

But a date? Oh, no. That was something else. What was she doing?

She had felt that wicked pull of attraction in the coffee shop and then working side by side and had forced it deep down. And she would have to do the same now, because the high tension wire that was pulling her closer and closer towards Scott would only lead one way—to heartbreak and pain.

She had learnt her lesson with Peter and dared not place her trust in a man like this again. She just couldn't risk being used then cast aside.

She wasn't ready to date anyone. Nowhere near.

'A dinner date? Thank you, but I don't think that would be a very good idea, Scott.'

'Elstrom Mapping just had a big success today. That's worth celebrating over hot food and a nice glass of wine. I might even run to a slice of birthday cake, seeing as I ate most of your brownies last Saturday night.'

Toni made the mistake of looking into those blue eyes. He was challenging her to take him up on his offer. And she didn't have any plans for her birthday.

'So this would be a business dinner? The hot food part does sound tempting.'

'If that is what you want. I can do hot food and talk business.'

She sniffed once then nodded. 'Okay, you're on. Throw in a tablecloth and cutlery and you have a dinner date. Not a fling, of course. Oh, no.' Then she opened up her smartphone. 'Do you want me to book somewhere?'

Scott covered her hand with his long clever fingers.

'Leave this to me. My treat. Let's make it a night to remember.'

Then he flashed her a cheeky wink and strode back to his office, his taut bottom teasing her with every step.

No messy complications and not a fling. Toni groaned to herself. *Right.*

CHAPTER NINE

SCOTT STOOD WITH his legs braced in front of the stone balustrade and looked out across the Thames to the south bank of the river. The early evening traffic was still fierce behind his back but he blocked it out and focused on the lights twinkling in the old stone buildings to the east that he knew led away towards the financial district and St Paul's Cathedral.

He was so engrossed at working through his mental map of the city he knew so well that it took a full second before he recognized the female voice behind him.

'Hello, handsome. I'm conducting a survey on people's favourite London walks and I'm keen to know what yours is. Do tell.'

Scott turned around just as Toni stepped forward. His reward for hanging around close to the busy road for the last ten minutes was the touch of her tantalising cold lips on his cheek. So, before she had a chance to move away, he grabbed her and kissed her on the side of the mouth. But pretended that he had been aiming for her cheek.

The kiss only lasted a second but he instantly felt the heat of her smile on his face.

'Cheeky,' she scolded, but then her eyes softened and that smile made him feel that it would have been worth running here through the snow.

He would love to touch her again and hold her in his arms. Instead, he held out his hand towards her and gave a low whistle.

'Hey, look at you, birthday girl! That colour is amazing!'

Toni held out the skirt of her long tailored Russian-style coat which was in a shade of bright cherry-red which he usually associated with Christmas decorations. And yet, with the black lace-up boots and black knitted hat pulled down over her ears, she somehow managed to look elegant and chic instead of too bright.

'You like? These boots are ancient but they're so warm and comfy I couldn't resist.'

'I like. Cute hat too.'

'Amy made it for me! We Baldonis are so talented.'

'It's a miracle that you stay so grounded and modest.' Scott laughed and when her gloved hand reached out for his, it seemed perfectly natural for him to mesh his fingers with hers. He couldn't recall the last time he'd held hands with a woman in the street. Alexa used to hate public displays of affection of any type. Maybe he should have taken a hint from that?

Either way, he liked this just fine. For the next few hours he was going to put aside the problems back in the business and do his best to enjoy himself.

'Now, about that walk,' he said in a casual tone. 'I have so many favourites it's hard to choose.'

'Um…I agree. I've lived in this city all my life and I still find parts which are completely new to me! It's astonishing.'

'Then here's a suggestion. Let's see where our feet take us. No particular direction or destination. Just free to go where we want. Then back to my very favourite place for dinner. And yes, hot food is on the menu.'

Toni gave his hand a squeeze. 'Somehow I suspect a map will be involved but that's okay. Lead the way, oh, great explorer.'

If someone had asked Toni to describe where they had walked and how long it had taken and what they had seen, she would not have been able to. Westminster Abbey was involved at one point and possibly Trafalgar Square because she did recall roaring with laughter about feeding bananas to the lions in London Zoo.

What mattered were the shared experiences of growing up in the same city. Their parents and their lives were so very different and yet the more they talked movies and music and the fun things they enjoyed the more connected she felt.

It was hard hearing Scott talk about his parents' divorce and how he and Freya had to struggle to keep in contact with their father when he'd remarried so quickly to a woman with a grown-up son.

With each step she felt that he was opening up to her, sharing his life and his love of the natural world. And all the time his hand kept a tight hold on her, taking her with him on the journey.

Scott was talking about his team of sled dogs and how he loved to watch them tug at the traces and take off on the trail across frozen forests and lakes. She looked up into his face and it was so alive and intense she could feel the heat and the passion for what he did burning in every word.

Maybe that was when a vague sense of unease started to creep into her thoughts.

What was she doing here? Sled dogs? Frozen lakes?

She didn't know whether to feel privileged that he felt able to talk to her about the precious things that mattered to him or overwhelmed by how quickly her fun birthday dinner stroll had turned into something much deeper.

He wanted her to know about his life, which was wonderful. But, if anything, it only made her feel inadequate and ill prepared for the new world she was facing in the coming months. She had never travelled or done any of these exciting things. The biggest challenge she faced every week was dragging Amy out of bed and now even that was gone. Lifting a camera might exercise a few arm muscles but that was it.

Their lives were so very different it wasn't funny. He had been to university and studied with the best in his field and she had barely survived college. She'd had Amy to take care of. But it didn't make it any easier.

It was foolish to compare her life with Scott's. They were such different people.

Problem was—she liked him more than was healthy.

A sudden flash of light snapped Toni out of her dream and she smiled at Scott as they strolled up to a road crossing. Suddenly a group of tourists ran across towards them and as she stepped left, Scott moved right and her gloved fingers slid from his. And she immediately missed that simple connection with the man.

Inhaling sharply and cursing her ridiculous crush, Toni quickly plunged her hand into her coat pocket so that Scott would not reclaim it, casually glancing from side to side.

Big mistake. Because in one step he had closed the gap between them and pressed his hand into the small of her back and then around her waist, holding her to him as they crossed the busy London road, which was a whirl of traffic and cyclists who apparently took red lights to mean go faster.

Her foolish heart relished that contact with the muscular

body that was so close to the surface of his relatively thin all-weather short jacket and how his hand felt on her back.

Crazy girl! It was madness to get her hopes up that they could ever be more than the casual friends that they had become.

The reality of their situation hit her like the cold wind blowing in from the river.

A fling. That was what he was offering her. A short-term, time-limited relationship.

Of course she was tempted. She had done nothing but think about his offer for most of the afternoon.

Stupid, really. She would be back at work in a week, and she knew that the diary would be filling in with lots of overseas trips. Scott was only here for six months and then he would be gone and she would probably never see him again.

But whenever she was within touching distance of Scott there was this tantalising tingle of something in the air that seemed to toss logical thought out of the window and re-place it with the idea that maybe he was the boyfriend that Amy had imagined that New Year's morning.

Decision time.

She could enjoy her hot dinner and thank Scott for a lovely evening with a polite kiss on the cheek and then tell him that her time at Elstrom had run its course. She had given him a week. So thank you very much but she needed to work on his painting and the house now. Be in touch when the plumbing was all sorted out and he could move in. Goodnight.

She glanced up into Scott's face as he cheerily chatted on about the time he'd tried to make a map of London at junior school out of tape and glue and poster paint.

He *was* a great man and it would be only too easy to fall and fall fast. She was already halfway there!

Or there was the other option. Take a huge risk and follow her feelings and play the fun friends with benefits card and live with the consequences. That was what she had promised Amy that she would do. Just another single girl having a good time with a great man while she had the chance.

Toni shivered deep inside her coat. This could be her only chance.

After what had happened with Peter she had struggled with her colleagues. Not one of them looked at her as a professional who could be their equal and over these past twelve months she seemed to have been offered projects where she was always going to be the assistant.

A strange idea crossed her mind and she pressed one hand to her forehead. Had she deliberately been accepting work where she knew that she would be in the background? That was all part of her training, wasn't it? To be the apprentice learning her trade from the experts.

Just as she had done with…her father.

Toni exhaled slowly as that thought rattled around inside her head and made her feel sick. She had slipped into the old pattern and not even realized it.

Worse. She had actually looked for those jobs, afraid to put herself forward as already trained and ready to work alone. Just as she had done with the paintings.

Scott chose that moment to laugh out loud and grin down at her.

She was a coward! Scott had given up the work he loved to come back to London to try to save his family business and his relationship with his father. He wouldn't let the Elstrom name go down without a fight.

A man like that was worth taking a risk on, no matter what happened.

Decision made.

Toni tucked her arm tightly into his elbow so that their hips touched as they walked but she didn't mind one little bit.

'Of course you do realize that your terrible secret is now out in the open, Scott Elstrom.'

Scott looked around as though shocked by the very suggestion and swallowed hard. 'Which one? I have so many.'

'No doubt. I was, of course, referring to the route march we have been following for the last few hours.' Toni counted out the vices on her fingers. 'Mr Scott Elstrom, Company Director.' She waved her fingers around. 'Not averse to a little travel on foot. Does not use a GPS, or at least I've never seen him use electronic mapping devices but, from what I saw this evening, he knows every highway, street and lane in this city like the back of his hand. Yes, Scott, I realise that you have walked me back to the same street as the Elstrom building. So that only leaves one question: how many maps of London have you drawn up over the years?'

He laughed out loud now. A real belly laugh, displaying his perfect teeth. 'Eight worth printing. Nine if you include the one I painted on my bedroom wall when I was seven years old.'

Toni gave an over the top gasp and jogged around in front of him, forcing Scott to look down at her when he replied.

'Wait just one minute. You can paint? When were you planning to reveal this secret skill? Or was it going to be a surprise?'

'Wax crayons and coloured pencils are my media of choice. So vibrant, you know.'

'Seriously?'

He looked at her for a split second, still laughing. 'Not a bit. I like technical drawing. Black lines using a straight-edge ruler and circles made from saucers and plates. Now that I am computerised, the survey company allow me to colour in the big bits but only when it's not important. They can always correct it later.'

Now it was Toni's turn to laugh, before she thumped him gently on the arm.

'You might have warned me this afternoon that we would be coming back here tonight! I spent ages choosing something smart to wear for my posh birthday dinner. I should have guessed that you would choose a restaurant close to home. Research—so important.'

'Absolutely. Which is why I'm taking you somewhere very, very exclusive. Think of it as your birthday present.'

'Exclusive! I like the sound of that. Even if I wasn't expecting a present. Is it very far?'

He smiled, and surprised her by sliding around behind her so that his arms were wrapped around her waist, holding her tight against him. She felt the pressure of his head against the side of her face as he dropped his chin on to her shoulder, lifted his left arm and pointed.

She pretended not to notice as his fingertips gently moved against her skin to flick the imaginary ends of her hair back over the collar of her wool coat, which was being warmed by Scott's hot body.

'For one night only, Elstrom Mapping has become Elstrom Fine Dining.'

'We're eating here! Wait a minute,' she said and tried to turn around to face him but the wall of muscle wouldn't move an inch. 'I asked for hot food and a tablecloth. Cutlery would be nice too.'

He brushed his stubbly cheek next to her throat so that when he spoke the words were whispered, hot and moist, in her ear. 'The way I want to kiss you right now might get us arrested. Especially when I have something hot and spicy waiting inside. Would you like to find out more? Was that a nod? Excellent. Let's go, birthday girl.'

Ten minutes later, Toni was starting to reconsider whether this was such a good idea after all.

'You didn't mention that walking upstairs wearing a blindfold would be involved,' she giggled. 'I hope you don't think that my birthday party was my usual kind of social event. Please, tell me where I'm going. If fluffy handcuffs come out I may run.'

Or perhaps not. But she didn't want Scott to know that!

His reply was a truly filthy low chuckle and he took even tighter hold of her waist and pulled her closer to him.

'That would spoil the surprise.'

He kissed her quickly on the top of the head, which made her giggle even louder. 'Get ready,' he whispered and their steps slowed. 'We've arrived.'

She felt him stretch forward and suddenly a very cold breeze whirled around her legs. Even the warmth of Scott's body pressed along her side couldn't block out that icy blast.

Toni took a tight hold of her bag but gripped Scott's hand tighter.

'Is this going to be an igloo-style dining experience? Because I have to tell you that I left my thermals back at the house.'

'Glad to hear it. Stay close. You'll be fine, trust me.'

One final squeeze of her hand and she took a step forward and cuddled even closer to Scott. Trust him! If he was planning to make her get up close and personal he was certainly doing a good job. It was freezing!

'Promise not to peek for ten more seconds,' Scott murmured and she could feel the heat of his breath against her neck and then the gentle tug of the ribbon covering her eyes being untied at the back and lifted away.

She carefully half opened one eye and then instantly blinked and stared in amazement, her eyes scarcely able to take in what she was looking at.

They were standing on a rooftop terrace with panoramic views across the London skyline. All the lights of the tall buildings and the winding curve of the River Thames were laid out in front of her on this clear, cold frosty night.

Every light twinkled and gleamed as though it had been polished diamond-bright just for her. And above her every star in the heavens was clear and sharp against the dark night sky, with only a faint glow from the city below.

It was as though she had been transported to her own personal roof garden overlooking London.

Scott took a step closer to an elaborate wrought iron railing and they stood side by side for a second, their breaths hot and fast and making faint clouds of mist in the cold air.

'Oh, Scott,' was all she managed to say, one hand pressed against her throat and the other still clutching on to his arm.

'Happy birthday, Antonia.' He smiled and wrapped his arm around her shoulders and hugged her. 'Happy birthday.'

Scott grinned down at Toni, who was standing next to him with a totally shocked look on her face, and was rewarded with a stunning smile that seemed to reach into his heart and unlock the heavy metal gates that he had constructed since Alexa.

There wasn't a hint of artifice or pretence in this girl's

smile and everything he had been through to make this evening possible suddenly seemed a small price to pay.

'Hey, birthday girl. Let's get you out of the cold.'

Holding tightly on to Toni's waist, he nudged her back towards the door and heard her gasp of delight.

'What? I cannot believe it.' She laughed up into his face and then looked back to the enclosed conservatory area of the roof garden, where he had set up his father's simple bistro table for dinner for two.

Electric lamps flickered on each wall, there were candles on the table and a blast of warm air welcomed them the second they stepped inside.

'My dad isn't too keen on the cold so he built this extension from his third floor flat out on to our roof garden when we were kids. We can be out of the wind here but still get the view.'

'Oh, wait until I tell Amy about this place.' Toni chuckled as Scott guided her into the half glass conservatory. 'It is actually warm and cosy. In fact I'm thinking of moving in. I love it. Want to make a trade?'

'Not quite. I have two heaters on full power just for you. And. Hot. Food.'

Scott guided Toni to her chair and watched her eyes pop with delight at the hot tray he had plugged in before he'd set out.

It only took a moment to pour her a glass of red wine and then one for himself.

'How about a toast? To lamb tagine and rice, made by the brilliant Moroccan restaurant down the street. A decent French red from the cellar. And good company. Cheers.'

'Good company,' Toni breathed as they touched wine glasses and then she took a sip and closed her eyes in pleasure as she savoured the wine. 'That's wonderful. In fact—' she gazed around the conservatory, taking in the tiny sofa for one and the bookcases and plants '—this is all wonderful. When you do exclusive, you do it in style, Mr Elstrom. I approve.'

'Then my work is done,' he said, smiling. 'I'm pleased you like it. The roof garden used to be one of my favourite places, even before this conservatory was built. There were fewer skyscraper buildings then and the stars seemed brighter somehow.'

He knew that his voice must have trailed away because Toni had stopped gazing out to the balcony and her entire focus was on his face. Her soft brown eyes flickered with amber and gold to match the colours in her hair and the connection between them pulled them tighter and tighter until her sweet gentle voice broke the silence.

'I would rather look at you,' Toni whispered as she got to her feet, slipped off her coat and crossed the few steps between them.

Her soft lips pressed against his and he tasted sweet red wine and all of the heat and warmth that he'd thought would never be offered to him again.

'I've been thinking about your offer,' she breathed, her gaze scanning his face as her fingertips traced gentle circles at the back of his head. 'And do you know what? I've changed my mind. In fact, I like the idea of a fling. Very…' she kissed his forehead '…very…' then his temple '…much.' And nipped the corner of his top lip with her teeth. Then her mouth lifted into the sweetest, cheekiest grin that he had ever seen. 'If the offer is still open?'

Her fingers cupped the back of his head as she angled her face and stepped closer so that her kiss could deepen and deepen, overwhelming and passionate.

Clutching hold of her soft sweater, Scott rode the wave of sensation until the tip of her tongue found his. And the rules went out of the window.

In an instant her lush body was crushed against his and his hands were exploring every inch of that frame as his mouth took over, nibbling her upper lip, then moving down on to her throat and then lower until his cheek found a home next to her breast.

Breathing became a second priority for a few minutes but he didn't mind in the slightest. He was perfectly content to hold Toni in his arms and use his mouth to give her pleasure, knowing that she wanted him as much as he wanted her.

It was time to find out just where this journey would take them.

'Scott... The lights have gone out.' Toni's words were murmured in between gentle nibbles on his ears and in the hollow of his neck.

'Probably a power cut,' he whispered and wrapped his arms tighter around her body, drawing it closer to him and trying to find a comfier position on the narrow wicker sofa. The moon was higher and lighting the room but the candles had burnt out an hour ago.

She nodded and then lifted her head. 'I can smell something burning. Is it our dinner?'

He chuckled for a full second before the smile dropped from his lips and with a deep groan of regret he took hold of Toni's hands.

'Nope. Not the dinner. That's the smell of electric cable burning. Sorry, Toni. I need to find out where the problem is.'

'Not without me,' Toni said and they pulled on their clothes and Scott dashed out of the conservatory and into his father's apartment, the moonlight at their backs guiding their steps.

Scott was right. The burning smell grew stronger the

closer they got to the main staircase and when they opened
the door to the apartment there was smoke in the hallway.

'I left a torch in the store room,' Toni called out as the
lights started to flicker. 'Just inside the door to the right.'

'On it,' Scott called back and took the stairs two at a
time and Toni saw the torchlight beam out only seconds
before all the lights went out and she was left in the smoke
and darkness.

'Scott! Are you okay?' she called out and blinked as
the torchlight blinded her.

'It's in the fuse box,' a dark shape called out through
the smoke which was so thick that she could hardly make
out his face. 'No time to grab your coat. We're leaving
and we're leaving right now. Before this whole building
goes up in flames.'

CHAPTER TEN

TONI SHRUGGED HER arms into an old cardigan belonging to Scott's father that she had found hanging on the back of a chair. But it was no good. She still stank of smoke. All of her clothes and certainly her hair and skin were dirty with soot and grime and no amount of rinsing her face could clear her eyes of that horrible gritty feeling.

She peeked around the corner of the main office and watched Scott direct the electricians to the totally burnt-out junction box which was the source of all of the smoke. No actual flames, thank goodness. That would have been truly terrifying.

Scott was even filthier than she was!

Hardly surprising. He had been amazing. Once he had known that she was safe outside on the pavement, he had dashed back into the service room with only a small fire extinguisher and the torch held between this teeth.

That was a sight that she was not going to forget in a hurry!

Her heart had been in her throat for the whole ten minutes until he had emerged, coughing and smoky. Through the smoke, it was obvious that the ancient electrical system had finally given up and had been totally burnt out and would need to be replaced.

The emergency electrician who arrived to make the

building safe gave them the bad news in the middle of the night. The whole building would have to be rewired to bring it up to modern safety standards. In fact he was astonished that this had not happened earlier. He had never seen anything this old still in operation. Anywhere!

Sitting in a coffee shop in their stinky clothing at first light was not exactly how she had imagined her birthday dinner would end. Scott wasn't going to get another up close and personal second viewing of her new burgundy underwear after all. Not tonight, anyhow.

It hadn't taken long for the shock to wear off and the real impact of the damage to sink in and they had sat in silence for a lot of the time, deep in thought.

Neither of them was stupid. All of that work had been wasted! And what would this mean for the financial plans for the building? Rewiring a two-hundred-year-old building was no easy task. Wooden panels and flooring were not designed to be easily removed and replaced. The work could take weeks!

Any plans to use Elstrom Mapping as a film location were officially on hold.

The true extent of the smoke damage was only really obvious when they braved the smell and went back in to open every window to try and clear the smoke. And this time there was no way that she would stay outside and leave Scott to do the work alone.

Her camera and the precious maps and charts had all been safely locked away in the mapping room drawers before she left the previous evening but other paperwork and some of the archive papers had been covered in smoke and smelt horrible.

It was heartbreaking to see this fine building that she had come to care about so much looking so wrecked and damaged.

Heartbreaking to see Scott trying to sound positive on the phone to Freya and the insurance company. Heartbreaking to sit with him and look at the damage and know how much work was needed to restore the greatness of this fine place.

And heartbreaking to know that she only had one more week to help him. Her boss at the media company had already emailed her twice to make sure that she would be at the airport on Monday morning for a flight to Madrid and then on to Athens a few days later to shoot a three-week commercial campaign for a housewares company. Her time at Elstroms was coming to an end.

What was she going to do? What could she do?

It was almost a shock to hear the phone ringing on Scott's desk and she jogged around and picked up the handset, just as Scott strolled into the room.

'Elstrom Mapping.' Toni said, trying to sound professional, but her throat was still a little hoarse to pull it off. 'Good morning.'

'Not from what I've just heard,' a high-pitched male voice replied. 'I need to speak to Scott right now. Is he there?'

Toni beckoned Scott to her and he gave a quick nod and stretched out his hand for the phone. 'One moment, please. Who shall I say is calling?'

'Just tell him it's Travis. He'll take the call.'

Scott must have seen the surprise on her face and his eyebrows creased together for a second before he put the phone to his ear, but that was nothing compared to the look of absolute rage that seemed to transform his face the second he heard the other man's voice.

'I wondered when you would call. It didn't take long, did it?'

Scott was on his feet, walking back and forth in front

of the desk with exhaustion only too clear on his face. But, as Toni sat back in his office chair, every word that exploded from Scott's mouth sounded like cannon fire.

'Sell the building? Now, why should I do that? A bit of smoke damage only adds to the character.'

Something Travis said must have upset Scott even more because suddenly he froze. 'How the hell do you know what my father wants? When was the last time you even spoke to him? Oh, yes, I remember. Just after you started screwing my wife. Forget it, Travis. I'm not selling. You're going to have to find some easy money somewhere else. Now, get off my phone. I have a business to run.'

Toni leant back as the phone came sliding across the desk towards her and she could hear the sound of Scott's breathing as he continued to pace with one hand pressed hard to the back of his head.

'So that was Travis. He sounded intense. It's amazing how quickly bad news travels.'

Scott threw off the thick leather gloves and tossed them on to the desk and stomped closer to her, but Toni stayed exactly where she was.

Scott was furious; when he spoke, each word was like a dagger stabbing at her forehead and penetrating her skull.

'Intense? Is that how you would describe Travis? Intense? You want to know about my stepbrother?'

Scott was almost spitting out the words as he said the name.

'That man hated the fact that his widowed mother married someone who he thought was totally beneath her in every way. Yes, that's right. My dad was a boring academic type who wasn't worthy to marry a woman with a title. How pathetic was that! And, even worse, the man had two children and expected him to play nice.'

Scott coughed. 'Travis broke up his mother's marriage

and then used every trick in the book to turn my family against me, starting with my father and then my wife, Alexa. And I cannot forgive him for destroying something I thought was special.'

Toni sucked in some air. 'You're still in love with her. I understand. Really. You can't just wipe away all of those years of your life that you spent together.'

'Ah, Toni, believe me—I'm over Alexa. But memories have this habit of kicking you when you're down. I haven't forgotten what it felt like to find my stepbrother and my wife together in the boardroom. And what they were doing on that table had nothing to do with forward planning, unless it was to find a contract which would keep me as far away from London as they could come up with. Alaska fitted the bill nicely.'

'Oh, Scott, surely you don't think that they planned it?'

'No, I don't think—I'm sure of it. Travis told me to my face on the day we first met that he was determined to have everything that I had. Well, he got what he wanted.'

Scott stopped pacing long enough to count out the list using his fingers. 'A controlling interest in Elstrom Mapping. My father gave his new wife half of his shares as a little wedding present and Travis a few more on his twenty-first birthday. All Travis had to do was persuade his mother to put the shares in his name, for tax reasons or some other excuse, and he had the shares he needed to sit on the board.'

'But surely he couldn't do that. You and your father ran the business.'

'And how could I forget my father? He made sure that there was always some excellent excuse why my father should attend some function Travis had organised instead of seeing me. And when I complained? I was being childish and jealous. So, of course, when the position for CEO came up? He took my job. The only job that I had trained for and wanted since I could read a map.'

'Oh, Scott, I can't believe it.'

'Believe it.' He paused a moment and shook his head and blew out sharp and fast.

'And then there was the lovely Alexa. She was the final trophy in his little collection. When he had Alexa he had the full set. He had everything he wanted. Everything he thought that I wanted. He had taken everything that mattered to me.'

Scott was pacing now like a caged animal. 'But Travis had forgotten something rather important. Where do you go when you have everything that you have ever wanted?'

Scott whirled, one hand in the air.

'I remember coming into this room on the day before I left for Alaska. Travis was sitting at the head of the table. Master of all he surveyed. And I looked at him and laughed in his face. Do you know why? He had no clue. None. About any of it. He didn't know how to run a business. How could he? He had shadowed me for almost a year but that wasn't nearly long enough. Sad thing was, Travis was clever enough to realise that he taken on too much too soon. But too arrogant to admit that he had failed.'

'So what did he do? After you left?'

'He did what any desperate fool does. He threw money at the problem. Brought in top consultants. Experts in new mapping technology. Anybody and anything that could give him a rope to hold on to so he could try and climb out of this pit that he had dug for himself and for Elstrom Mapping and have someone else to blame when it all went wrong.'

Scott gazed out of the tiny squares of mullioned glass on to the busy London street and his voice dropped to a sad whisper.

'My father came back from Italy with Freya and walked
in the front doors to find the bailiffs were already here to
unplug all of the ludicrously expensive computer systems
that Travis had ordered and never bothered to pay for or
train anyone to use.'

Scott looked at Toni over one shoulder then turned back
to gaze at the city street.

'Travis was gone. Resigned. Walked out. Leaving Freya
and my father to try and sort out the chaos that he had cre-
ated and left for other people to deal with.'

'Oh, no. That's so cruel.'

'Cruel and irresponsible,' Scott agreed. 'But if you're
looking for someone to blame for my father's poor health,
don't look to Travis. Start with me. Because I saw it coming and did not do one thing to stop it.'

'What do you mean, you saw it coming?' Toni asked as
she stepped closer to Scott so that she could see his face.

'It was common knowledge that we desperately needed
to invest in new mapping and survey technology. That was
why I had spent three months studying the alternatives
and putting together a proposal which would have taken
us into the next generation of mapping.'

Scott turned and gazed at the imposing chair at the end
of the table. 'I stood here and spent an hour going through
the detail. Freya loved it. But she was the only one. Alexa
and my father sided with Travis. He couldn't wait years.
I wasn't being adventurous enough. I needed to wake up
and be more experimental. I was not the man for the job.'

The pain in Scott's voice was so intense that Toni rested
her hand over his in support and for a moment his gaze
focused on her. 'I walked out, Toni. I was so angry and
bitter that I wanted Travis to fail and for the world to see
it. Why should I stay and try and save the business when
my father had chosen to put his trust in Travis instead of

me? Let Travis bankrupt the business. Then they would see who was wrong and who was right!'

Scott gave a low shuddering sigh. 'Not something I am proud of. He brought out an ugly side of me which I didn't know existed.'

'That was what he wanted to do, wasn't it? Make things so impossible that you had to leave him in charge of the company.'

Scott flashed her a closed mouth smile. 'Clever girl. He goaded me into it by forcing me to choose whether to stay and work with him or take off. So no, Travis Brooks is not my favourite person in the world. And now he's back and he needs money. The question is—what will he do to get it this time? My ex-wife soon outlived her usefulness and he moved on to the next wealthy woman a year later. He had no use for her any longer. And I cannot forgive the man for that.'

Toni paced up and down the parquet floor several lengths, her head down but her gaze was wild as she mentally worked through the question and tried to come up with an answer.

'Did Travis keep his shares in the company?' she asked, blinking.

'Not all of them,' Scott replied. 'Alexa was an expensive luxury so he sold a few to Freya when he needed some money.'

'Freya? Yes, of course. Neutral territory. I'm beginning to get the picture. One last question.' She licked her lips. 'What about Alexa? Does she still have a say in what happens to Elstrom?'

'Alexa wanted half my shares as part of the divorce but when she saw what was left after Travis was left in control, she changed her mind and walked away with the home that we had made together as final settlement.'

He strolled forward and tented his hands on the table. 'I can see where you're going with this. My dad might be ill but he has handed over his control of the company to me. Travis has some shares, but I control the decisions now. What I say goes and he had better get used to that.'

'Travis could still fight you.'

'I expect him to.'

Scott gestured towards the stairs. 'This fire is nothing. Just a small temporary setback. Your location scout won't even know that things have changed. I'll make sure of that.'

He broke into a strange and slightly scary grin. 'This is round two, Toni. Now it is his turn to feel excluded. And this time I get to win.'

'Win?' she repeated. 'So this is a battle. Oh, Scott. Don't you see what he's doing? Travis is pulling your strings again. Making you play his game and by his rules all over again.'

Toni stood in front of Scott and pressed the palms of both of her hands flat against his chest. 'Don't let Travis manipulate you into doing something you will regret, Scott. Because, if you do, he will have won.'

That caught Scott's attention. 'What do you mean—won?'

'You told me on my first day in this office that you had come back to save the family business from losing everything. But now I'm wondering if that was the only reason. Was it to do with Alexa and Travis?'

'You don't know what you're talking about, Toni. It has been a hell of a long night. Why don't you head off home and get some sleep and I'll catch up with you later?'

'No, Scott. I need to hear this. Please. Tell me now and I will never mention it again. Why have you come back to work for Elstrom? You told me that it was about your family legacy. I understand that better than you could know. But I'm beginning to think that there is a lot more to it than that. Why are you here, Scott? Why did you agree to come all the way from Alaska to save an old wooden building and a few rooms of maps and charts? Was this to spite Travis and get retribution for taking your place in your family?'

Scott gazed at her with a stunned expression on his face, jaw slack and his eyes dancing.

Then, just as quickly, he shook it off.

'Right now I am a lot more interested in making this building safe to work in. The junction box is fried and I don't intend to spend a minute longer than I have to on Travis when there is so much work to do.'

'All I am asking for is the truth. That's all.'

'The truth? You want to know the truth? Why don't you ask Travis? He will tell you his version of the truth. Oh, yes. Golden boy Travis could even convince my own father that I was responsible for throwing my wife at him. I neglected her, you see. Left her all alone while I was out working on every mapping project I could find. According to Travis, all that work had nothing to do with trying to save the company. It was all because I couldn't stand to see Travis in charge of Elstrom Mapping instead of me.'

He pushed both of his hands flat against the brick wall and closed his eyes for a second before speaking into the distance, his voice low and harsh and intent.

'And do you know the worst thing? He was right. I couldn't stand to see Travis at the head of the boardroom table with all of those portraits looking down at the back of his head. So yes, I took too many trips overseas to win some new business to pay for the extravagant lifestyle that my father's new family was living. There was no one else doing the work to bring in new business and for once I was determined not to see it go down with the crazy plans for expansion that Travis and Alexa came up with between them without even bothering to ask me first.'

'Was it so very bad?'

'Need you ask? It was a disaster. My father trusted them to turn the business around. Clever academic business degree Travis was going to rescue the company and bring it into the new technological age of map-making.'

Scott shook his head and coughed low in his throat. 'He had so many grandiose plans and no clue about what he was doing. So yes, I went out looking for new business, but don't you dare tell me that it gave him permission to seduce my wife behind my back and laugh about it to my face.'

'I would never do that,' Toni gasped. 'And I'm sorry that you had to go through that. It was inexcusable and cruel. I know…I know how it feels when someone you love betrays you.'

'You know? You have no idea what it felt like to walk into the boardroom and find my wife with Travis. You have no idea at all. Because it was one of the few times in my life when I understood why people commit crimes of passion. He was very lucky that day that I chose to walk out and leave the two people who I thought were my family to rot.'

The sound that Scott's fist made when it hit the wall made Toni jump with shock. 'No, Toni. You only think that you know. You don't have any idea at all.'

CHAPTER ELEVEN

EVERY ONE OF Scott's words hit Toni like a slap across the face and she flinched as though he had struck her.

She felt instantly overwhelmed by what had happened a year ago on her birthday.

An event which she had pushed firmly away as past history.

Her breath caught in the back of her throat and she gasped at the sudden flash of memory. Pain surged through her and she collapsed down on the hard wooden chair, her legs like jelly and unable to take her weight. Suddenly she felt sick and tearful and pathetic.

'You are wrong, Scott. I do know. Because exactly the same thing happened to me.'

'What are you talking about? How can the same thing have happened to you? Have you ever been married?'

'No. But I had a boyfriend who I trusted and cared about more than I should. We were together day and night for almost three months working on a documentary in France together. I thought I knew him and that he loved me and wanted to be with me. I was wrong. About both of those things.'

'No—' Scott started to speak but she held up one hand '—let me finish.'

She had to get it out and explain or she would go mad.

'I had worked like crazy for weeks to finish the filming and editing before the deadline and it still wasn't done. Peter was doing the networking and keeping the client happy; I was working the cameras. We were a great team. Then he asked me to help him out. He had been invited to a family wedding and really wanted to be there but that was going to be impossible unless we finished the final studio work that week. Could I help him by finishing it on my own? Then we could meet up back in London in time for my birthday that weekend.'

Toni dropped her head back. 'Of course I said yes. He was my boyfriend. I would do anything for him. I worked for forty-eight hours straight to make the deadline. And it was great work.'

She sniffed and gave a low laugh. 'The problem was, it was so good that the client offered me a free ride back to London on the company jet. Fantastic, I thought. I'll pop around to Peter's apartment and drop off the equipment then take a day's holiday to sleep. But something weird happened on the flight. The client asked if I could get hold of the talent agent for Peter's girlfriend. He had completely forgotten to ask Peter and they were looking for a lingerie model for another campaign. They were such a handsome couple!'

A low chuckle turned into a half cry. 'I started to tell the client that he was wrong and that I was his girlfriend but suddenly things started to click together in my mind. The fabulous clothes in Peter's wardrobe which he claimed belonged to his sister who used the apartment. The telephone calls he took at all hours of the day and night from clients. And the texting. The constant bloody texting, day and night. It all made sense.'

Her voice faded away. 'There was no family wedding. That was just an excuse that he had made up to get rid of me. Peter was having a clothes optional dinner for two with his Brazilian girlfriend when I turned the key and walked in on them in the shower.'

Even moistening her lips could not make the words come any easier.

'I am sorry. I had no idea.'

'Why should you? I keep these things to myself,' Toni replied. 'He used me because I was convenient and trusting and I fell for it. That hurts and it never completely goes away, does it?'

His answer was a small shake of the head.

Toni closed her eyes and luxuriated in the warmth of his body pressed against her side and, without thinking of the consequences, she leant sideways against him, daring to push the boundaries that they had set in the bedroom.

His left arm snaked around her waist and Scott drew her even closer to his body.

She could feel the pounding of his heart under his smart blue shirt as she pressed her fingertips to the soft fabric which separated his skin from hers, only too aware that one thin layer of mightily creased cardigan wasn't perhaps the best outfit she could have chosen to rescue smoke-damaged documents. She must stink of smoke.

Strange. Somehow, that didn't seem important any longer.

Who was she kidding? Scott meant more to her than any man she had ever known. She had never told anyone about that day. Not even Amy knew the real truth. Until this week she would never have thought it possible that she could forge so powerful a bond to this amazing man and feel that friendship and connection back in return.

Peter had been her lover and her colleague and for a few idyllic and heady months in one of the most romantic cities in Europe she thought that they had a future together. But, looking back, she knew now that Peter had never been her friend. Real friends didn't use one another.

'Tell me what you need me to do,' she whispered. 'I have to go back to work in a week but I have loads of pals who would be happy to help. We can bring a team in and start the clear-up. We can turn this place around in a week. You wait and see.'

She could stay this way for ever and not regret it. But, just as her head lolled back against the chair, she sensed his mood change, as though someone had opened the window wider and allowed a cool breeze into the room.

His arm slid away from behind her back and he moved, just an inch, then more, and their bodies slid apart, slowly at first then swiftly as Scott stepped sideways and bent over the paperwork on the table.

The shock of being separated was like a physical blow to Toni's poor heart. But it was the look on Scott's face that truly startled her as he turned to face her.

Desire, anguish, self-reproach and unmistakable desire. For her.

She had not been mistaken after all.

The way his hand had started to seek hers when they were out, the way she caught him looking at her when she least expected it, and the kiss on the roof terrace the night before had been real. The gentleness of his mouth on the nape of her neck which turned her legs to jelly had meant as much to him as it had to her.

And she didn't know whether to grin and shout in glee while she had the chance, or be patient and let him take the lead.

This was why, when he did speak, the words he used touched her heart and made it weep.

'A week? You think we can clear up this mess in a

week? Somehow, these past few days I had forgotten that you have your own life and another job. Oh, Toni.'

His finger stroked her cheek from her temple down to her chin. 'I can't do this, Toni. I thought a fling was what I needed—hell, what we both needed. But you're a lovely woman and any man would be honoured to have you in his life and we both know that I will be back in Alaska in a few months. It wouldn't be fair on either of us to make promises we can't keep. No matter how much we would like things to be different. You should go back to your work and make it the success it deserves.'

Well. That answered her question.

Two choices. She could accept what he said and let him go with a smile on her face or she could do something mad and challenge him.

Just the thought of not having Scott in her life sent a cold shiver down her back. He was hers and nobody else's. And she hadn't even realized that until this moment. She didn't want to lose Scott Elstrom. She couldn't lose him, not now, not after all they had shared together.

She wanted Scott and she wanted him badly enough to fight for him.

'Can't do what, Scott? Be friends with me? Like me and want to spend time with me? Want to hold me in your arms? Is that what you can't do, Scott? Please tell me the truth because I'm starting to get confused by what your body is telling me and the words coming out of your mouth.'

Before Toni realized what was happening, Scott had crossed the few steps that separated them and had wrapped his hand around the back of her neck, his fingers working into her hair as he pressed his mouth against hers, pushing open her full lips, moving back and forth, his breath fast and heavy on her face.

His mouth was tender, gentle but firm, as though he was holding back the floodgates of a passion which was on the verge of breaking through and overwhelming them both.

She felt that potential, she trembled at the thought of it, and at that moment she knew that she wanted it as much as he did.

Her eyes closed as she wrapped her arms around his back and leaned into the kiss, kissing him back, revelling in the sensual heat of his body as it pressed against hers. Closer, closer, until his arms were taking the weight of her body, enclosing her in his loving, sweet embrace. The pure physicality of the man was almost overpowering. The movement of his muscular body pressed against her, combined with the heavenly scent that she knew now was unique to him alone.

It filled her senses with an intensity that she had never felt in the embrace of any other man in her life. He was totally overwhelming. Intoxicating. And totally, totally delicious.

And, just when Toni thought that there could be nothing more pleasurable in this world, his kiss deepened. It was as though he wanted to take everything that she was able to give him and without a second of doubt she surrendered to the hot spice of the taste of his mouth and tongue.

This was the loving warm kiss she had never known. The connection between them was part of it, but this went beyond friendship and common interests.

This was a kiss to signal the start of something new. The kind of kiss where each of them was opening up their most intimate secrets and deepest feelings for the other person to see.

The heat, the intensity, the desire of this man was all there, exposed for her to see when she eventually opened her eyes and broke the connection. Shuddering. Trembling.

Then he pulled away, the faint stubble on his chin grazing across her mouth, as he lifted his face to kiss her eyes, brow and temple.

It took a second for her to catch her breath before she felt able to open her eyes, only to find Scott was still looking at her, his forehead pressed against hers. A smile warmed his face as he moved his hand down to stroke her cheek.

He knew. He knew the effect that his kiss was having on her body. Had to. Her face burned with the heat coming from the point of contact between them. His heart was racing, just as hers was.

'Is that the way you usually silence women who ask you tough questions?' Toni asked, aiming to keep her voice casual and light as she tried to catch her breath. And failing.

He simply smiled a little wider in reply, one side of his mouth turning up more than the other, before he answered in a low whisper. 'I save it for emergencies. And for when I need to answer tough questions.'

Scott pulled back and looked at her, eye to eye. 'You have to know that it is killing me to even think about leaving you here when I head back to Alaska, but that is where I belong. Freya will be back tomorrow to help me with the cleaning and organising the media companies and she's happy to do it, but she doesn't need me, Toni. There is no work for me here. You deserve a lot better than a part-time lover.'

He was nuzzling the side of her head now, his lips moving over her brow and into her hair as she spoke. 'Do I? I think that is the nicest thing that anyone has ever said to me.'

'And I mean every word. Your life is here, where you have a brilliant future as an artist and photographer. I can see it now.' His hand scrolled her name in the air. 'Portraits by Antonia Baldoni. It is going to be magic. Who knows, I might even come and have my photograph taken.'

'No need, Scott. I have all the photographs in the world. But they don't come close to the real you.'

Scott rested his forehead on her for one more second before he stood back and held out his hand. 'It's been a delight working with you, Miss Baldoni. Good luck in your future career.'

Then he turned and strode away from her, back to the second floor and the sound of sawing wood and drilling. Leaving her sitting there in her smoky clothes and hair with a broken heart. Bereft and alone. And already missing him more than words could express.

CHAPTER TWELVE

SCOTT STROLLED INTO the boardroom at Elstrom in the bright March sunlight and was immediately leapt on by Freya, who gave him such a warm hug that all of his fears and apprehensions for this day instantly vanished.

Holding her at arm's length, Scott moved his head slowly from side to side to check that they were the only two people in the room.

'I know that Dad is still in Italy because I spoke to him this morning. But where have you hidden Travis? I thought his ugly face was bound to turn up at any boardroom meeting where money would be involved. Do I need to look under the table? That's the only place he would be out of reach of my fist.'

'Now don't be like that,' Freya scolded and wagged a finger at him. 'Travis sent me a very sweet email yesterday, telling me that he had decided to leave Elstrom behind for good and move on to pastures new.'

Freya must have caught the look in his eyes because she gave him a quick nod. 'Yes. That's right. Travis has sold all of his shares. And no, before you ask, I don't know who he sold them to. It certainly wasn't anyone in the family because I asked around. So don't give me that look. Who knows? It might be someone who has a real interest in the business. Think positive for once!'

'Positive! Right. Well, I can't say that I'm sorry to see him go. But I don't like the idea that we have an unknown investor. That makes me nervous.'

Freya hooked her arm through the crook of Scott's elbow and tugged him towards the back of the room.

'Then here is something to put a smile on your face.' She nervously licked her lips and Scott saw it.

'What's going on? I thought that you'd called me here for a board meeting?'

'I have.' Freya nodded. 'With my office manager hat on, I can tell you that everything is going splendidly, the building is booked for the next two years with more enquiries coming in every day and the finances have never looked rosier. The full report is on your desk. There. Done. Now, on to much more exciting stuff.'

She stepped back and slowly angled her head towards the wall behind the head of the table. 'Notice anything different?'

Scott rolled his shoulders back and followed her gaze, then blinked.

The full-length portrait of his uncle had been moved to the left, creating a gap which was occupied by a tall gold frame which matched the other portraits perfectly. What was inside the frame was covered by a plain grey dust sheet held up by a piece of tape, hiding the painting below.

It took a second for his brain to register what he was looking at.

'Toni finished my painting. Wow. I wondered about that.'

'Wonder no longer. That girl works fast! I have already seen it and paid the rest of her fee,' Freya whispered, then stepped to one side and kissed him on the cheek. 'This is your very own personal unveiling. Call me later. Love ya.'

With that, Freya swung her handbag over her shoulder

and strolled casually out of the room, leaving him standing there with his back against the table, staring up at the dust sheet.

Something close to nerves ran across his shoulders. This was so ridiculous! This was only paint on canvas. Why did he need a personal viewing?

He took a couple of calming breaths. Who was he kidding? This was paint brushed on to one of her father's canvases by the same clever fingers which had stroked his face and made him feel alive only a few weeks earlier. Until he blew it.

She had probably made him look like his grandfather. Complete with morning dress, sideburns and a handlebar moustache.

He deserved the worst.

Forcing the air from his lungs in one short blast, Scott tugged on the dust sheet and then gathered it up on to the floor.

Only then did he stand up, lift his chin and focus on the painting hanging on the wall in front of him.

What he saw took his breath away and Scott quickly pulled out a chair and collapsed down into it. Suddenly his legs were not quite as steady as they should be.

His portrait was astonishing.

Toni had painted him standing at the mullioned window of the office. His legs were braced and he was wearing cold weather gear and the fur-lined boots he had arrived in from Alaska. It was a side view and his left hand was resting on a wide decorated chart spread out on the mapping table in front of the window. Survey equipment and a dog sled harness were right there, on top of the map.

But that was not where the eye was drawn to. Scott's gaze was riveted by the expression on his face. He looked tanned, unshaven, with swept back hair but, with his chin up and his back straight, he looked the equal of any of the other Elstrom men captured on these walls. Strong, powerful and in control. Even down to the grey in his beard and stubble.

But this portrait was different.

Toni had seen something in him which nobody alive had ever truly noticed before.

Yearning. It was in the way his blond eyebrows came together in concentration as his eyes stared out of the window where gentle snowflakes blurred the hazy outline of the tall buildings opposite Elstrom. His mouth was curved into a small warm smile as though he was dreaming of somewhere else. She had painted his eyes a shade of blue that he knew from his reflection in the mirror every morning. The exact perfect shade.

Tears pricked the corners of Scott's eyes and he left them there.

Freya was right. This painting was intensely personal. Every single brush stroke screamed out to him that the hand that had painted his image cared about him so deeply and intensely that it was impossible to conceal.

It was a love letter in the shape of a painting.

Toni Baldoni was in love with him.

A bubble of happiness popped up from deep in his chest and he scrubbed his chin a couple of times. Men like him rarely got second chances and he had never imagined that it could happen twice.

Damn Toni for showing him how wrong he had been. No way was he going to lose his chance of love again!

Leaping to his feet, Scott saluted the strong and intelligent-looking man in the painting before whirling around and striding to the door. 'Wish me luck. I have ten minutes to work out how to tell Toni what I feel. *And it had better be good!*'

* * *

'Oh, rollers,' Toni grunted through gritted teeth as a great splodge of white emulsion paint dropped off the end of her paint tray and on to the leg of her painting overalls. She didn't mind the paint; she was used to that. It was the wet patch she was not too keen on.

No time to get changed. She was determined to finish the studio walls today and that was precisely what she was going to do! It was the third coat and the last. From now on, the studio walls were going to reflect back every bit of the natural light she needed if she had any chance of working the way she wanted.

For the past three weeks Toni had filled her days and sometimes her nights with the perfect challenge. Transforming the Baldoni studio into a space which she could use for new clients and new portraits. She didn't need a photographic studio on the high street. Not any longer.

The first things to go were the cracked paint trays and old chewed paintbrushes which she knew that she would never use. She had broken up the old wooden cracked picture frames and battered shelving and used them as firewood. That little splash of linseed oil really helped warm the old stone walls. Papers went for recycling. Same with the dried-up paints and oil cans.

It was as though working on Scott's portrait had unleashed a cleaning demon which had been waiting inside to get out.

The portraits that her father had hung on the terracotta-coloured walls were the last things to be taken down. His hoarding of every receipt and invoice had actually come in useful for once and in three cases the client who had sat in this very studio so many years ago had been delighted to pop in and buy a copy of their portrait from the artist's family and at very good rates.

The nice thing was, the moment they'd taken a look at Scott's painting on the easel, they had been so delighted that they'd wondered if she might be available to paint their granddaughter or son who had just received a wonderful promotion at work.

Three new commissions in three weeks.

She would never have thought it possible.

Scott Elstrom had a lot to answer for, in more ways than one! No matter how many late nights she worked or how physically exhausted she was at the end of the day, Scott still filled her thoughts with dreams of what could have been and what had been lost.

It only took one glance at his portrait to take her instantly right back to Elstrom Mapping and the man who owned it.

It was gone now. Freya had collected it yesterday. All boxed up and packed away.

So why did Scott's face still flood her mind even now, halfway up a ladder with her arms stretching up to cover the walls with white paint?

Stepping down from the ladder for a moment to check for dark patches, Toni was suddenly aware that there was a cold draught from the kitchen but she was sure that she had closed the back door.

Wiping her hands, she stepped into the kitchen and was suddenly aware that there was someone standing in front of her.

It was Scott.

In the flesh.

He was here. Standing in front of her. All tall and gorgeous and clean and handsome and so attractive she could happily have dived into those blue eyes and warm arms and not come up for air.

The masculine strength and power positively beamed

out from every pore and grabbed her. It was in the way that he held his body, the way his head turned to face her and the way he looked at her as though she was the most fascinating woman he had ever met, and oh, yes, the laser focus of those intelligent blue eyes had a lot to do with it as well.

He was so close that she could touch him if she wanted to. She could practically feel the softness of his breath on her skin as he gazed intently into her eyes. The background noise of the radio she always played at full volume when she worked seemed to fade away until all of her senses were totally focused on this man who had captivated her.

She couldn't move.

She did not want to move.

There was an awkward gap and just then her resolve gave way and she felt that she simply had to say something—*anything*—to fill the silence. 'What are you doing here, Scott? What do you want from me?'

Her words blurted out in a much stronger voice than she had intended, and she instantly warmed them with a small shoulder shrug. 'I thought that you were travelling?'

Scott straightened his back and lifted his chin. 'What am I doing here? Well, I thought that was fairly obvious. I'm here to thank you for the portrait.'

Freya!

'Do you think it is a good likeness?' Toni asked as casually as she could.

'Perfect. It's me. All of me. Outside and inside too. I don't know how you did that with paint but you did. Clever girl.'

'It's in the blood. But I'm pleased that you like it. That means a lot.'

He tilted his head slightly to one side and gave her a lopsided grin which made him look about twelve years old.

And her poor lonely heart melted all over again.

She smiled back, her defences weakened by the wonderful charm and warmth of this man she cared about so very much, who was standing so very close and yet seemed beyond reach.

'What have you been doing with yourself these past weeks?' Scott whispered. 'Travelling the world with that camera of yours?'

'Actually, I've been working on my own projects, right here.' She waved her right hand in the air and looked up at the white-painted ceiling. 'I thought that I might stay in one place for a while.' Her voice quivered a little. 'In fact, I decided to take a year's leave from the media company and focus on painting for a while. See where it takes me.'

Scott glanced quickly over her shoulder before turning his gaze back to her face. 'You've worked wonders. It looks amazing.'

His fingers traced a line along her chin from ear to throat. 'My portrait is stunning. You should be very proud of your talents, Toni. I believe you have it in you to achieve amazing things with your work. Photographs, painting. It's all part of your creative genius. You're destined for wonderful things, my girl.'

His girl?

'Oh, Scott, I've been such an idiot,' she whispered.

His reply was to cup Toni's head between his hands, his long fingers so gentle and tender and loving that her heart melted even more.

'You were right, Scott. I did need to paint your portrait. And it wasn't just for the cash, although it has been very useful. It was more than that. A lot more.'

Her head dropped forward on to his chest so that when she spoke her words were swallowed up in the warmth of his fleece shirt.

His reply was a low sigh of contentment as he wrapped his arms tighter around her back and drew her even closer so that she was totally encased in his loving embrace.

'Ah. She finally admits that I am a genius in all things. Happy days.'

'You don't get everything right. You thought that I couldn't understand what it was like to see the Elstrom heritage slip away from you. But you are so wrong about that.'

Words and feelings whirled around inside her head and her heart so fast that she thought she might pass out if it wasn't for Scott's strong arms holding her upright.

But how could she explain without giving away a secret that she had sworn to her parents that she would never tell anyone unless she had to?

Toni closed her eyes and listened to the sound of Scott's heartbeat. It was strong and clear and it beat for her and only her. She was certain of that now.

It was so hard to step back from Scott but she could still feel his arms around her as she whispered, 'I need to show you something. Okay?'

Sliding away, she took hold of Scott's hand and with one quick smile she led him into the bedroom and gestured for him to sit on the bed.

'If this is a lingerie display I may have to call Freya and tell her that I'm missing dinner.'

With a quick chuckle, Toni shook her head. 'Sorry to disappoint you, but this is more of an art display.'

Toni knelt down next to her bed and tugged an old battered leather suitcase out from underneath. Taking a long juddery breath, Toni slowly pressed the metal sliders away and felt the lid of the suitcase spring up as the pressure was released.

Suddenly exhausted, Toni sat on the floor next to the

suitcase with her back pressed against the bed and her legs outstretched in front of her.

Slowly and with shaking hands, she lifted the suitcase lid and sat for a few moments in silence. Staring back at her was the sweet smiling face of the nine-year-old Amy. It was the last portrait that she had ever painted and signed under her own name. Lifting up the thin wooden light canvas, Toni smiled and stroked the edges as a freckle-faced happy girl with long hair and a turned-up nose and missing teeth grinned back at her.

When she finally found the words Toni was speaking more towards the picture than to Scott but she knew that he was listening.

'Every brush stroke of this painting was a delight. Our annual holiday had been in Cornwall for a couple of weeks the summer after I turned seventeen and we had all gone down to the beach for the afternoon. That was a rare event in itself. My father hated the sun and would much rather have stayed inside working on a commission he had to deliver the following week. It had been going too slowly and he couldn't seem to concentrate on the work so Mother had suggested that he take the afternoon off.'

Toni smiled to herself. 'It turned out to be a wonderful day of happy relaxed laughter and fun and sheer pleasure. Not too hot. Not too windy. Perfect blue skies and golden sandy beach. It was only natural that I should take some photographs of Amy and my parents. I had never intended them to become sketches or paintings. But somehow the moment I lifted the camera and pointed it towards Amy everything changed. I called out her name...Amy turned towards me.'

Toni flicked both hands in the air. 'And bam. Just like that, I knew that the photograph would be wonderful. Not just good. But special and amazing. And that feeling was so astonishing and overwhelming that I started to cry.'

'Cry? Why were you crying? Didn't that make you happy?'

'Yes. Amazingly, wonderfully happy. But it was sad at the same time. All my life I had been focusing and training on one thing—to be a painter and true artist like my parents. And in that moment, looking down that camera lens, I realized that it was all for nothing. Because I had never once felt that way with anything that I had painted. Not once. I could paint professionally any day of the week. And that's not being immodest. It was the truth. But taking that photograph changed everything.'

She glanced over her shoulder at Scott and smiled through the tears that were streaming down her face. 'Until then I was Antonia Baldoni, little daughter of Aldo and Emily Baldoni. Painters. Artists. But that moment made me realize that I could take everything I had learnt and apply it to creating portraits and paintings with more than canvas and paint. I had found my passion. Just like you found yours.

'I was so excited that I was jumping up and down and laughing and crying at the same time and generally making my parents fearful that something terrible had happened. I couldn't wait to tell them. I thought that they would be so excited that I had found the artist in me.'

'Oh, Toni. I know where this is going. My poor girl.'

Her head dropped. 'It came as a bit of a shock to realize that everything I believed about being part of a family of artists until that second was completely wrong. They were not excited for me at all. In fact they were horrified. Speechless with shock and horror. They felt it was a betrayal of my legacy. And then there was my dad's work…'

Her hands got busy lining up the edges of sheets of her

sketches and notebooks inside the suitcase. She focused on the gold-edged papers so that when Scott shuffled closer she could pretend that a collection of ragged teenage work was far more interesting than the man whose trouser leg was only inches away from her shoulder.

'What about your dad's work?'

She pulled out a sketchbook and started casually flicking through it, not ready to look into his face.

Her fingers paused at one particular drawing and she ran the pad of her forefinger down the edge of the smooth paper she liked to work on.

'Have you ever heard of the studio system? No? The old masters used to train young artists as a way of making some extra income. They all did it. The more famous you were, the more parents were prepared to pay to have their children study with you and work in the studio.'

She lifted her chin and gestured towards the next room where the art supplies were kept. 'I remember a time when there were always three or four art students from the local college hanging around, making tea and preparing canvases and now and again my dad would let them make sketches on a sitting with a client. So he could critique their work. Show them how to develop the idea into a painting. Maybe even work on a background for one of his portraits. If they were very good.'

Tears pricked the corners of her eyes and she wiped them away with the back of her knuckle.

'Fame is a fickle thing, Scott. One day everyone loves your work and the next? You're history and nobody wants to hire you because the exciting new style is all the fashion and who needs their portrait painted? That's why cameras were invented.'

She felt his body lift from the bed as the hard springs

squeaked in protest and suddenly Scott was sitting on the floor next to her, his back so tall against the divan.

His left hand slid sideways and as she glanced down all the weight and strength that Scott possessed seemed to flow through those fingers as they meshed with hers.

'He resented you for leaving him.'

She nodded. 'I was his last apprentice. The student who was going to make her mark in the world and show the art establishment just how powerful fine painting could be. I was going to lead the next generation of Baldoni portrait painters proudly forward.'

Her head dropped and she picked up Amy's portrait with her left hand. 'I painted this when I was seventeen. By then I was working every night after school in the studio and doing nearly all of my dad's canvases. My weekends and every day of the school holidays were spent in that studio.'

She shook her head and blew out hard. 'I was his apprentice so it made sense for me to be there for the sittings so that I could paint the backgrounds and clothing on his portraits. He always worked on the fine detail. Afterwards. But as I got older and he got more disillusioned and depressed about how much photography was taking over, I found that he was leaving me to work on the few commissions that were coming in.'

Scott breathed in through his nose. 'You were doing the work. Weren't you? You were painting those amazing portraits and he was passing them off as his work. Oh, Toni.'

His fingers squeezed hers for one last time then slid away and moved around her waist so that he could draw her to him.

'It didn't feel like that,' she replied and rested her head on his shoulder. 'I loved the work and wanted to learn everything I could. This was my real education. School work

was not important in the least. Not like it was to Amy.'
She chuckled deep in her throat. 'It was a bit of a shock
finding out that we had a scientist in the family. Her idea
of drawing was a flow chart and computer spreadsheets.'
Then she swallowed down a lump of guilt and regret.
'But of course that put even more pressure on me to fly
the flag for the family and carry on my legacy. So when I
announced that I was moving to photography…it hit them
hard. So very hard.'

'What did you do?'

'What could I do? For a while they did everything they
could to try and make me change my mind. That I was
making a huge mistake and throwing away my career and
that people would start commissioning portraits again. I
just had to carry on and learn my craft and be patient and
it would all work out.'

She glanced quickly over one shoulder towards Scott,
who was breathing hard and fast on to the top of her head.

'Ever wondered what proud artists do when they don't
have any work coming in? They borrow on the only real
asset they have left. This house must have been mortgaged
and re-mortgaged four times. A commission comes in,
they pay some of the loan off, then the money runs out
and they borrow again and…I learnt the hard way that
putting your home at risk to pay the gas bill is a stress-
ful way to live.'

'Your family? Other relatives? Couldn't they help out?'

'Oh, no. My father was a stubborn man and he would
never have contacted his Italian side of the family. A Baldoni would never sink so low. So he dropped his prices
and offered to paint children and local people. Said that it
was his way of being generous.'

She chuckled and sniffed. 'They needed me to work
and work hard to create commercial pictures they could

sell quickly to bring in some income. And that is what I did. Nights and weekends. There are children around here with a genuine Baldoni portrait on their walls!'

'Did you sign them?'

'Of course I did. *A. Baldoni*. They didn't know that it was an Antonia Baldoni and not an Aldo Baldoni work they were buying—why should they? Everyone called me Toni. The local mayor would have been very upset if he knew. I think he is still bragging about that painting to every visitor to his official office.'

She wiped away one tear and whispered, 'Very upset. Seeing it was the last one that my father claimed to have painted before he died. It's his claim to fame.'

'How did it happen?'

'A train crash in Italy. It was June. They had been invited to a family reunion and scraped together the rail fare with some sort of excuse about them hating flying. It was…brutal to lose them both at the same time. Horrible, really. I was just about to leave school…'

Her eyebrows squeezed together tight. 'And that was the end of my hopes and dreams. How could I go waltzing off to my dream course in New York to study photography when I had a sister to take care of? So I stayed in London and went to college when Amy was at school and did the best that I could with grants and loans. And we worked it out. The two of us together. I got a job with a media company which meant that I could stay in London as much as possible. It was fine. Until I got a call from a certain Freya Elstrom.'

'My sister is a well-known troublemaker.'

Toni nodded. 'I thought that I was ready to put all of the painting behind me. Amy and I spent Christmas sorting through so much rubbish and clutter so I could get the house ready to decorate and rent out. The only room I didn't touch was the studio.'

She flashed Scott a half smile. 'The plan was to donate the unused canvases and equipment to the local school. Amy's art teacher would have taken everything if she had the chance. But somehow I couldn't bring myself to do it. You were my excuse.'

'I like to be useful.' Scott smiled back.

'Amy is no fool. She saw through my little pretence straight away so I convinced her that this was going to be my last portrait. Ever. One more painting and I would be done. End of an era. But then I met you. And my world has never been the same since.'

Her hand swept out, her eyes hot and fierce, and she tapped the heel of her hand against the hard planes of his chest. 'I blame you for everything, Scott Elstrom. All of it. I was happy to leave painting behind until you came along. My life was all planned out. Neat and tidy. Until you walked into my birthday party and blew me away. I have done things this month that I never imagined possible.'

She pressed the fingers of both hands hard against her forehead. 'Because do you know what I have done? Exactly the same thing as my dad did. I have borrowed money on my house to invest in Elstrom. And it is all your fault!'

CHAPTER THIRTEEN

SCOTT STARED AT Toni for a few seconds before he finally made the connections.

'It was you! You bought the shares from Travis.'

He looked to one side for a second as though his mind was trying to process what she had done. But when his gaze locked on to her face it was full of warmth and utter astonishment.

'You put your home on the line. For me! That is the most amazingly generous thing that anyone has ever done for me. And I don't even know where to start to thank you. Those shares will give me...'

'Your freedom,' Toni interrupted. 'I wanted you to be free of the past, Scott. You are an Elstrom. Your destiny is to be travelling the world exploring trade routes to some distant shore, not sorting through old pamphlets. You can do what you want now, Scott. Stay. Go. Be with who you want, where you want. All I am doing is returning the favour. There is no need to thank me.'

'I cannot believe that you did that for me.'

Gulping down her fears about how this proud man might react to her working behind the scenes without his permission, Toni looked up into Scott's face and what she saw there wiped away any doubts.

'You know why I did it. I love you, Scott Elstrom, and a girl will do anything for the man she...'

Toni never got to finish her sentence because her lips were far too busy being crushed by Scott's hot mouth.

She reached up and stroked his cheek, her eyes brimming with tears.

'I haven't stopped thinking about what you said. And you were right. This is the biggest risk of my life, your life, anyone's life.'

She breathed in, her heart thudding so loudly that she suspected he must have heard it. 'I know now that I will always love you, Scott Elstrom, and it doesn't matter where you are in the world. And if that means that I have to let you go, to be free to do your work—' she licked her lips '—then that is the way it has to be. I want to be with you. Love you. If you still want me to wait for you?'

Scott stood very still, staring at her, and she bit her lower lip in fear. She might have just made the biggest mistake of her life but this was the way it had to be and she was prepared to be turned down.

'I could be away for six or seven months at a time, you know,' he told her gently, his voice low, sensual and intimate.

'Probably longer. But that is the way it has to be. I didn't fall in love with an office clerk; I fell in love with you. I have to let you go and do what you have to do, wherever that is, so that you can be true to who you are. Because, just maybe, we can still get back together one day. I love you, Scott, and that is not going to change whether you're in Alaska or the Himalayas or down the road.'

Scott didn't answer, but she slid her fingers from his so that he could caress her face, his gaze scanning from her grubby nose to her roughly tied back out-of-control hair.

'You love me, but you are willing to let me go and do this work which means so much to me? Is that right?'

She nodded, too afraid to trust her voice. 'As long as you are somewhere in this world loving me, then I shall be fine. My heart will be your beacon home to my love. You don't even need a map. You'll always know where to find me. Apparently, there are people who still want their portrait painted so I'm staying put after all. Who knew?'

'Then there's only one answer to your question. Looking back these past few weeks, I can see just how low Alexa and Travis took me. I couldn't believe that the woman I loved was capable of doing that to me. To us. I was in love with my wife, Toni, but she didn't love me. That's hard to come back from. So my answer is no. I don't want you to wait for me.'

Her heart caught in her throat but he pressed one finger on her lips and smiled, breaking the terror. 'You see, I'm not as brave as you are. As soon as I saw that portrait this morning, I knew that I couldn't leave the woman I have fallen in love with without trying to come up with some options.'

He grinned at her and slid forward so that both of his hands were cupped around her face as tears pricked her eyes. 'I love you way too much to let you go. I need you, Toni. I need you so much. Nothing else comes close. What would you say if I told you that Freya and I have come up with a plan which will make it possible for me to work out of London for the summer months?'

She shuddered out a chuckle of delight and relief. 'I would say, *Yes, please,* and then I would ask how you have managed it.'

'Freya has been fielding enquiries from location scouts from TV and movie companies all around the world. Your idea worked, Toni. It worked brilliantly. We already have bookings for most of the year and part of the next. Elstrom Mapping is safe for the next five years and I have a job as a location actor any time I want one.'

Scott took both of her hands in his, his voice suddenly full of life and excitement and enthusiasm. 'There was one extra condition before I signed my new contract with the survey company in Alaska. I told them that I would only do it if I could bring my girlfriend with me to Anchorage in October so that she could see the Northern Lights for herself. After all, she is a professional artist and one of the Baldoni family. She deserves first class travel all of the way.'

'Your girlfriend—' She breathed out the words, tears pricking her wide eyes, scarcely daring to believe what he was saying.

'You have given me the greatest compliment a man could wish for. You offered me your love and your confidence and the freedom to live my life. I never imagined I would find a woman who could love me as much as I loved her. I am not going anywhere without you and I mean that.'

Scott's voice faltered as he pressed his forehead to her flushed brow.

'I have travelled all over the world, Toni. I might have kidded myself that it was for work, but the truth is harder to accept. I needed to prove to myself that I was not a complete failure and that I hadn't let my family down when I walked away from the firm.'

'Oh, Scott. It was never your fault. Just as it wasn't mine. I know that now. You *have* made a difference because the man I love has given his life to his family. And I know how many sacrifices that takes.' She was stroking the hair back from his forehead now, her fingertips moving through the short curls as she stared into the depths of those stunning eyes.

'I have never felt such an overwhelming sense of belonging than in those few days I spent with you. I didn't even realize that I was looking for it. Your heart is my beacon home. Wherever you are is where I want to be. Bring me home, Toni. Bring me home.'

He knelt in front of her as he whispered in a husky intimate voice that she had only heard before in her dreams, 'I love you and want you to be part of my life, Toni. If you'll have me?'

Toni looked into a face so full of love that her heart broke.

'Oh, my sweet darling. How can you ask that? You have to know that I love you. I will love you for the rest of my life. You are the centre of my world.'

She choked with emotion as Scott stood, swung her up into the air, her arms linked behind his head, whirling her around and around until her feet connected with the chair.

In an instant Scott lowered her to the floor, grabbed her hand and threw her over his right shoulder as though she weighed nothing.

He was almost in the middle of the street before she managed to wriggle free and, holding hands, they pulled and twirled each other around and around, heads back, laughing and shouting in pleasure, thick snowflakes falling around them, before collapsing into each other's arms, their heads pressed together into a passionate kiss.

It was picture perfect.

* * * * *

A sneaky peek at next month...

MODERN
tempted ™

TRUE LOVE AND TEMPTATION!

My wish list for next month's titles...

In stores from 18th July 2014:

❏ The Heat of the Night — Amy Andrews

❏ The Morning After the Night Before — Nikki Logan

In stores from 1st August 2014:

❏ Here Comes the Bridesmaid — Avril Tremayne

❏ How to Bag a Billionaire — Nina Milne

Available at WHSmith, Tesco, Asda, Eason, Amazon and Apple

Just can't wait?

Special Offers

Every month we put together collections and longer reads written by your favourite authors.

Here are some of next month's highlights— and don't miss our fabulous discount online!

On sale 18th July   On sale 18th July   On sale 18th July

Save 20%
on all Special Releases

Find out more at
www.millsandboon.co.uk/specialreleases

Visit us Online

0814/ST/MB487

THE
CHATSFIELD®

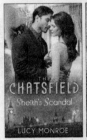

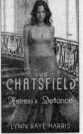

Join our *EXCLUSIVE* eBook club

FROM JUST £1.99 A MONTH!

Never miss a book again with our hassle-free eBook subscription.

★ Pick how many titles you want from each series with our flexible subscription

★ Your titles are delivered to your device on the first of every month

★ Zero risk, zero obligation!

There really is nothing standing in the way of you and your favourite books!

Start your eBook subscription today at www.millsandboon.co.uk/subscribe

Make it a summer to remember with the fantastic new book from Sarah Morgan

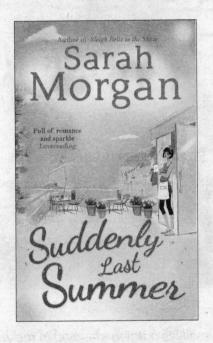

Author of *Sleigh Bells in the Snow*

Sarah Morgan

Full of romance and sparkle
Lovereading

Suddenly Last Summer

Fiery French chef Elise Philippe has just heard that the delectable Sean O'Neil is back in town. After their electrifying night together last summer, can she stick to her one-night rule?

Coming soon at millsandboon.co.uk

Anouska Knight's first book, *Since You've Been Gone*, was a smash hit and crowned the winner of Lorraine's Racy Reads. Anouska returns with *A Part of Me*, which is one not to be missed!

Get your copy today at:
www.millsandboon.co.uk